CHARLES, WITH LOVE

CHARLES, WITH LOVE

SYDNEY WINWARD

Charles, With Love

Cover art by LLewellenDesigns.com

Published by Silver Forge Books

Paperback 978-1-960461-06-3

http://www.sydneywinward.com

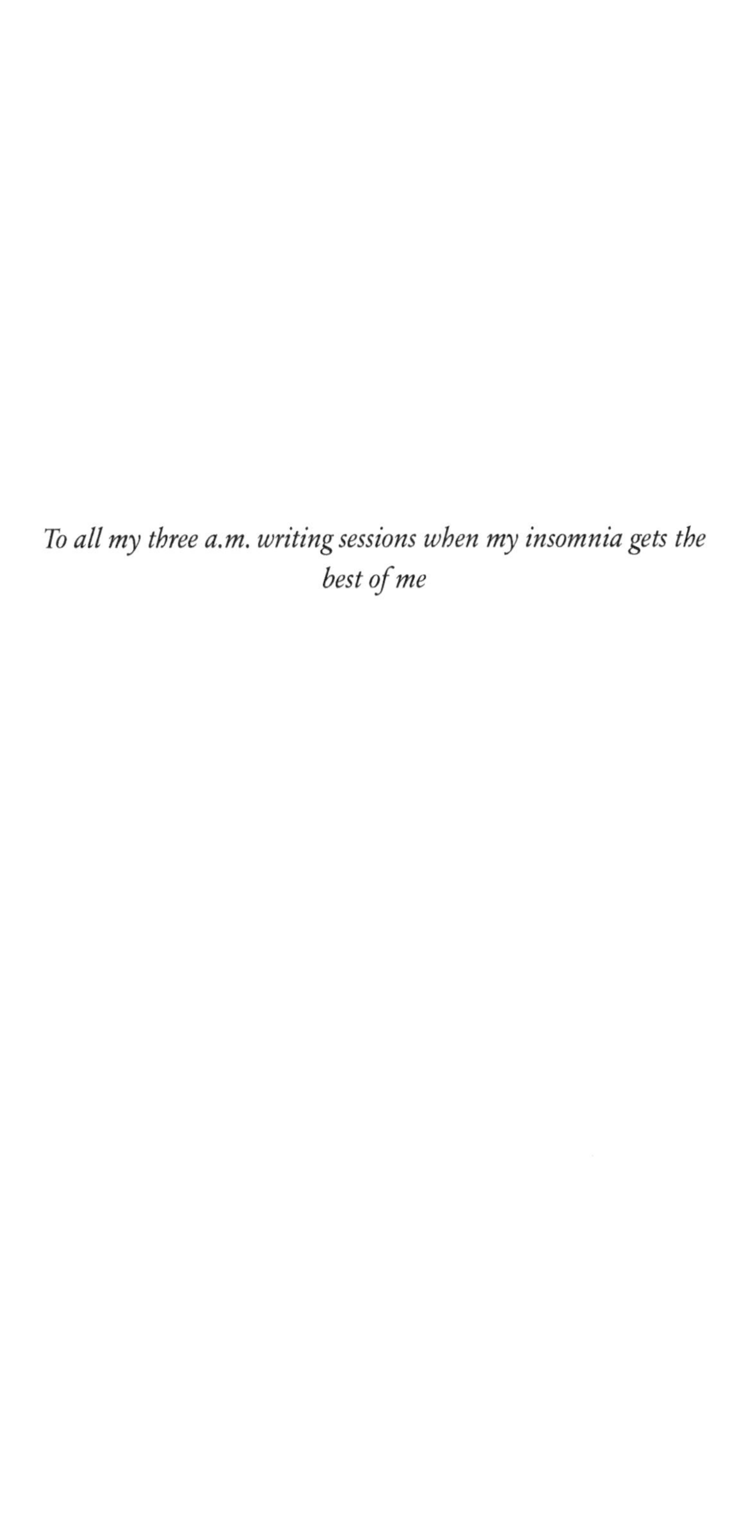

To all my three a.m. writing sessions when my insomnia gets the best of me

BOOKS BY SYDNEY WINWARD

The Bloodborn Series

Bloodborn
Bloodbond
Bloodscourge
Bloodbane
Bloodcurse
Bloodheir

Sunlight and Shadows Series

A Breath of Sunlight
A Taste of Shadows
A Glimpse of Music
A Kiss of Embers
A Balm of Healing

Letters to Love Series

Yours, Sterling
Forever, Mirabelle
Always, Ivette
Charles, With Love

Lord Death Series

A Waltz with Lord Death

Novellas

Through Wylder Meadows
Root Brew Float
On Silver Wings
Bloodmoon
Bloodvow
Selkie

Chapter One

Six years ago, Charles Lockwood had many dreams and aspirations and plans for his future. What he hadn't imagined was finding himself riding behind a dreary carriage in a dreary line of dreary guards, pretending he cared about the princess's dreary life as she hid away for hours on end during their long, never-ending journey from Leonia to Amoria.

He scrutinized the black carriage ahead, a sun painted on each side with yellow and orange paint—the symbol for Leonian royalty.

Behind him, a guard grumbled to another guard. "How long is this going to take? Surely, we're at least halfway there."

"We've only been on the road for five hours." The second guard hacked up a cough and spat to the side of the dirt path. "We've got twenty more to go. Not counting the stops."

Charles kept his mouth shut, knowing he'd glean more information by staying silent than chiming in.

"Princess Isobel hasn't stopped once," the first guard said with a huff of annoyance. "Seems she's more than thrilled to meet her betrothed."

"The man is on his deathbed," the second guard scoffed. "No doubt he's trying for an heir before he dies. Otherwise, the throne will go to some unknown relation."

The relentless late-afternoon heat beat upon his helmet, trapping the warmth inside the metal prison. Perspiration dripped down his neck, and he broke the illusion that he was a statue wearing guard attire by lifting his hand to scratch beneath his chin. A week's scruff brushed his fingers, giving him a more rugged appearance than his usual clean-shaven nobleman look.

He scratched his chin again, patiently reminding himself, *It's all for the assignment.*

He'd been through worse. Acting as a guard to a snobby princess was one of the easier assignments given to him.

Of course, he'd never actually met the princess, only seen her at a distance. But the rumors floating around the Leonian castle were that the girl was insufferable, she was selfish, and she was a snob.

Thank the heavens, he thought to himself as a gray cloud passed overhead, blocking out the sunlight and tackling the relentless heat. A shiver ran down the length of his spine at the sudden change in temperature. But he'd always preferred the colder weather over the hot and dry climate Leonia often boasted of. At least in Amoria, they'd be at a higher elevation in the mountains, giving him a bit of reprieve for as long as he planned to stay in the kingdom.

His horse whipped its tail through the air, its ears turning back as if he, too, had tired of the long journey already.

He leaned forward and patted the animal reassuringly on the shoulder with a black leather-clad hand. The creature nickered and threw its ears back once again.

Surreptitiously, Charles glanced to each side of him through the eye slits in his metal helmet. Two dozen soldiers rode alongside him, both in the front and rear of the royal carriage. Only the princess and her traveling companion resided inside, while her personal guards rode directly beside the carriage.

It was quite a bit of fanfare to protect the princess on the long journey. But it was better to be overprepared than underprepared.

Using the pressure of his legs only, he guided the horse a step to the side to overhear another conversation murmured in hushed voices while keeping his attention on the procession in front of him.

"I'm telling you," the man said quietly to the other, "something's not right about her. I haven't heard her speak in an entire week, and we all know she likes the sound of her own voice."

"She's about to marry an old man." Charles could almost hear the eyeroll in his voice. "Of course, she's quiet."

His attention shifted to the carriage once again. Why hadn't she stopped for a break? Unless...there was a reason she needed to arrive at their destination quickly.

The horse nickered again, and he pulled his gaze away from the carriage and to the antsy creature. This was a new mount for him, and he was unfamiliar with its quirks. But if he wasn't mistaken, the creature seemed nervous.

His gaze scanned the endless forest on either side of them, peering closely at the shadows moving across the ground as the clouds overhead shifted from their position in the sky. A bend in the path ahead prevented him from seeing beyond the tree-covered hill. But he doubted wolves or another predator would stalk them with so many in their party.

The rolling wheels of the carriage grew louder in the antagonizing silence. He shifted in his saddle to give him a better vantage point over the endless rows of metal helmets. The weight of his weapons moved with him—a sword on his hip, a dagger strapped to either thigh, a bow slung over one shoulder, and a quiver of arrows on his other shoulder. Of course, he carried several knives tucked on his person as well.

He was a firm believer in carrying plenty of weapons and keeping them on himself at all times whenever possible. Because the only person he could trust was himself. As far as he was concerned, everyone else was the enemy.

Again, his horse nickered and side-stepped, fighting against the reins. He frowned and tried to gain control.

What has you spooked? he wondered quietly.

He glanced up to find several other horses protesting the reins, and his attention diverted to the ground. Snakes, perhaps? It wasn't unheard of for the slithery creatures to make a nest on well-traveled roads.

Someone made a choking sound, and Charles' gaze shot up. Only for dread to encompass his entire body. A crossbow bolt protruded out of one of the princess's personal guard's throats. Blood rushed down his chest, and a moment later, he tipped to the side and fell off his horse, smashing into the ground.

By the time others registered what happened, Charles already spun his horse around with the intention to escape the ambush. If he died or got caught, he would find himself in even deeper waters than a simple arrow to the throat.

But just as he broke free of the procession, men in leather armor and helmets dropped down from the trees with war cries as they drew their weapons and began their slaughter.

Screams lifted into the air. Horses cried out with pain or fear. Bolts continued raining down from the boughs, dropping soldiers like bees in a cold climate.

Keep calm, he silently ordered his horse as he kicked the creature in another direction.

But the enemy blocked his path of escape, forcing him to draw his sword. He held the weapon in one hand while maintaining his grip on the reins with the other. Without hesitation to protect his own life, he swung and stabbed and parried, maneuvering the weapon like an expert extension of his arm.

A blade swung toward his neck. He lifted his sword and diverted the enemy's weapon over his head, using the momentum of the attack to his advantage. With a swift movement, he unsheathed the dagger at his thigh and thrust it into the other man's chest.

He turned his mount just as the enemy started to fall off his stolen horse, but he didn't stay long enough to watch him hit the ground.

After dispatching two more enemy soldiers in what appeared to be an ambush of at least thirty men, a gap emerged just large enough for one man and a horse to fit through. He started toward it but froze at the sound of a feminine scream.

He couldn't stop himself from glancing behind him. Near the carriage, the dark-haired maid servant lay in a pool of her own blood. Another woman with blonde curls and a lavender gown rested on her hands and knees, ducking her head from the swipe of a blade.

Charles internally groaned at himself as he kicked his mount in the opposite direction through the chaos surrounding him. Princess Isobel was not his concern. But he couldn't just let her die.

An arrow whizzed past his face, a blur of motion visible through the helmet slits. With heart pounding, he continued forward with sword drawn into the chaos of screams and shouts, smashing weapons and bloodshed, all while keeping his eye on the princess.

Someone dressed in leather crossed his path in a quick, disorienting movement. Charles barely caught the edge of the man's weapon to prevent it from slicing his knee. But he wasn't fast enough to block the mace aimed at him before it smashed into the side of his head with a deafening roar, hitting his helmet hard enough to knock him off his horse. He landed on the ground in a thunder of crashing metal.

His head spun. His ears rang. The side of his head pulsed with agony. Something warm and sticky dripped down his neck.

But he forced himself to roll out of the way of the same mace swinging downward at him. His metal armor weighed him down considerably. But rather than getting sliced in half by an enemy weapon, he gritted his teeth and pulled through it.

He rolled to his feet and withdrew both daggers. Swinging. Slashing. Stabbing. Until the way ahead cleared enough for him to spot a man with his sword raised above his head, his sword pointed downward.

The princess raised a flinching hand.

The man lifted the sword higher.

Charles reacted on instinct as he threw one of his daggers with all his might.

Just as the man started to stab downward, his dagger whizzed through the air and pierced the man in the chest. The soldier stumbled backward, his sword falling out of his grip and clattering to the ground.

Not wasting another moment, Charles sprinted toward the princess, ripped his dagger out of the man's chest, and sheathed it before latching onto the woman's arm.

She screeched and fought against him, kicking and hitting him in an attempt to break free. He shouted at her to stop, but his words were lost in the deafening chaos surrounding him.

Anger and frustration coursed through him when she punched him in the stomach. But he reckoned it hurt her more than it hurt him when he wore armor, and she didn't.

He grabbed her kicking and screaming around the waist and hoisted her into the saddle of a nearby frightened horse trying to flee for its own life.

A weapon glanced off his armor from behind. He stumbled into the horse, which frightened it even more into leaping forward into a terrified gallop.

His boots slid through slippery dirt and slick, bloodied mud as he fought to find his footing while desperately holding onto the pommel of the saddle as the horse dragged him behind. Finally, he managed to dig his foot into the stirrup and swung his leg up and over the side of the horse.

With the princess sitting in front of him, her screams quieted by deep gulps of air, he reached past her and snatched the reins before they managed to evade him completely. He steered the horse away from the main road and into the forest to his left.

Archers lying in wait in the boughs shot at him with their crossbows. A bolt glanced off his armor, and another whizzed past his face.

He kicked the horse faster all while holding tight to the princess around her waist, trying to keep her smaller body tucked safely against him.

An overhanging branch whipped him in the face. The stumble of the horse's hooves nearly unseated him. Shouts echoed behind him as the enemy tried to catch up with them on foot.

His pulse thundered through his ears when they approached a knee-deep stream. But rather than trying to find a way around it, Charles urged the horse to enter the water.

Water kicked up around them, drenching their clothing as they traveled upstream for a good number of minutes before they exited the river on a rocky shoreline to help hide the horse's tracks. He located a small game trail and kicked his mount as fast as it could carry them down the dirt path.

A larger river took them upstream once again, and by the time they exited the water for a second time, the princess shivered uncontrollably against him, and the horse wheezed with each breath.

But he pushed the horse even more. Because if they stopped, it could mean their deaths.

Thankfully by now, the princess seemed to understand he was not the enemy. Well, at least to her knowledge. And she sagged exhaustedly against him.

They rode until the sky began to darken overhead. And only when riding in the dim light became dangerous did he stop the horse within a small clearing surrounded on one side by large boulders and the other by forest.

He listened for several minutes for any sounds of pursuit. But when he found none, fury burst through him as he angrily dismounted, wincing when the action pained his head. He tried not to hobble after a long day in the saddle as he tied the horse's reins to a low branch to give it the freedom to graze the grass at the base of the tree.

The moment the princess slid off the saddle, Charles spun on her. "Could you do nothing more than mope over your lost companion?" he snarled, trying to pull the helmet off his head. But the dent in the side he'd received from the mace made it impossible to pull it free. "You sat there and did nothing. You could have at least tried to save yourself."

The woman sniffed and turned her head to the side, the waning light only managing to make her face look paler than a sheet of parchment. "What do you expect of me?" she asked in a soft, sweet voice. "Weaponless. Taken by surprise. I was not ready for an ambush. And it seems as if neither were you or your comrades."

"*You*," he pointed down at her and glowered, only wishing she could see his glare through the helmet stuck fast to his head, "are not my problem. I should have let you die."

The words were callous and cruel, and he knew it. But a strange woman, who was not his charge—not truly—was not worth his own life.

The princess blinked fast, clearly holding back tears through her scathing glare she directed back at him. She poked him in the armored chest, the touch dainty enough that he could barely feel it through the layers of metal.

"*You* are a heartless fortune seeker who doesn't care about anything but the money you were offered for being my escort."

"Heartless?" He laughed and shook his head. "What reason do I have to care about you? Just because you are some high and mighty daughter of a king, you think you've won the hearts of everyone who looks upon you?"

"And what about honor?"

His lip curled in a snarl. "There is no such thing."

He stepped away, but the shift of his weight caused her to lose her balance. She tried to catch herself with a foot forward but cried out in pain before her leg collapsed beneath her. She crashed into him, and he barely managed to catch her beneath the elbow to keep her from hitting the ground.

A quiet whimper escaped her mouth, followed by a wince. She didn't try to pull out of his grasp. Didn't try to right herself. Almost as if she…couldn't.

Charles sighed, his gaze lifting toward the sky as he tried to find the faintest sliver of patience. "You're injured."

Now was about the time when he could eat his words. She likely hadn't been able to escape because of the injury.

"But you could have at least tried," he grumbled quietly under his breath as his hand moved to her waist. In a quick movement, he hefted her to her feet and supported her weight as he helped her toward a nearby boulder. She limped at his side, and when her leg collapsed beneath her again, he held her steady around the waist and slowly lowered her onto the mound of rock.

Carefully, he reached for the foot he assumed to be injured, and he was almost surprised she didn't stop him to comment something about honor and chivalry. He slipped her shoe off her foot, and she hissed when he pulled her stocking down to reveal a nasty purple bruise on her swollen ankle.

"The carriage rolled over my foot," she explained in a tight, evenly controlled tone despite the tears shimmering in her eyes.

He released a long breath as he stared at the swelling and the bruising. This was not the job he was hired to do. In fact, the princess was low on his list of priorities. Not his concern.

"Let's get you dry," he finally said as he stood, abandoning her on the rock as he scoured the area for kindling and firewood. "You won't last the night if you're cold and shivering."

He felt her gaze following him as he gathered what he needed and stacked the wood and kindling in the middle of the clearing. But he never lifted his head to meet her gaze. It wasn't easy, anyway, when his heavy head was bogged down by the weight of his helmet.

When he shifted his head the wrong way, the helmet dug into him. He inhaled sharply when a jagged piece of metal cut into him behind his ear, and more blood dripped down his neck.

"Are you injured?" the princess asked.

Charles refrained from answering lest his anger over the near-death incident spark a blaze within him once more.

Instead, he focused on starting a fire with the flint and steel he found strapped to the horse's saddle bags.

He struck the flint against the steel. A shower of sparks skittered across the ground. Another spark lit up the growing darkness. And finally, after a few more tries, the kindling caught fire.

He attempted to blow on the small embers, but the air hardly managed to escape the small airways in the helmet. With a huff, he quickly gave up and fanned the sparks with his hands instead.

The feat took longer, but finally, a fire sparked to life, beginning its slow climb up the logs he placed in a triangular fashion.

Sure that the fire would grow rather than recede, he focused his attention next on the horse. He took the bit out of its mouth to give the creature a reprieve for the night and then unstrapped the saddle and placed it on the ground. A single bedroll was rolled up and secured to the side of the saddle, and he couldn't help but huff again. He wouldn't last the night without warmth. And she *definitely* wouldn't last the night without it, either.

The woman was small and dainty and rather entitled to her honor and chivalry. He wanted nothing to do with her. But he could decide her fate in the morning.

A groan escaped him as he unstrapped the armor from his chest first and set it beside the saddle on the ground. Next, he relieved himself of the armor protecting his legs and arms. Bruises and aches marred his own skin beneath his guard's uniform consisting of a gaudy yellow. He shucked the ugly tunic to the side, leaving him in a pair of brown trousers and a loose, white shirt.

"What's your name?" the princess asked, breaking the stillness of the popping fire and crackling flames.

He only grunted. He'd simply give her a fake name, anyway, so it truly didn't matter for her to know.

"How old are you?"

Another grunt.

After a pause, she commented, "You can take off the helmet."

"Oh, can I now?" Sarcasm leaked from his voice as he tapped on the uninjured side of his helmet. "It got bashed in during my daring rescue of a helpless princess. It's not going anywhere."

She crossed her arms. "Are you always this sour?"

He frowned and turned away from her with the sudden realization of *why* he disliked her so much.

She was royalty.

And she was a woman.

His stomach twisted in agonizing knots as his mind flashed back to the night that had changed his entire life. The reason why he was where he was now. The reason he avoided women as if they were plagued with disease.

Rather than answering, he remained quiet as he laid out the bedroll beside the fire. It was large enough for two if they squished together. But quite honestly, he wanted nothing more than to put as much distance between them.

He touched her only long enough to help her sit on top of the bedroll, closer to the fire, to warm and dry the clothing she wore. He found a handkerchief inside a saddlebag and used it to wrap her foot. It likely wouldn't help the injury much, but it was enough for now.

When his need for space and peace won over his desire to make it through the night without keeling over, he made himself a bed beside the horse, where the creature lay on the grass, knees tucked beneath itself. Hopefully, it wouldn't roll over on him during the night. But the warmth it offered was better than the warmth the princess offered.

"I thank you for saving my life," she said, breaking the stillness of his peace.

His shoulders slumped as her words brought him back to the darkest day of his life. The pain. The *agony*. He avoided women because it hurt too much to breathe in their presence.

"Think nothing of it," he finally said in a quiet tone.

The last thing he managed was to toss a bag of dried fruit and nuts toward her, which landed on the bedroll beside her leg. Thankfully, enough food was packed in the bags to last a grown man two weeks on the trail if he ate sparingly. It would last the two of them a week at most. That was if another critter didn't decide to steal it when they weren't watching.

He attempted to make himself comfortable even when lying on his helmet was torturously unbearable. Through the slits in the helmet, he stared up at the darkening skies, his arms folded over his chest for warmth.

Despite the warmth from the nearby fire and the heat from the horse, the chill of loneliness and heartache still sank into his bones without menial tasks to keep his mind busy. The loneliness transitioned into anger. He latched onto it and held it close. Because without it, he knew he would surely fall apart.

Chapter Two

Emmaline Blythe woke to the sound of grunting and swearing and the slamming of metal. She bolted upright into a sitting position, blinking against the bright morning light as she tried to make sense of her unfamiliar surroundings.

She sat within the warmth of a bedroll, the remains of a fire a few paces from her covered feet. A wall of boulders lay behind her while the sprawling forest spread out in front of her.

A horse nickered softly from where its reins secured it to a branch. And both of them watched as the soldier who had saved her life bashed a rock against his helmet as if in an attempt to free his head from within the confines of the warped metal.

"Infuriating piece of sh—"

She interrupted, "Let me help—"

"I don't *need* any help," he growled, and she felt his scathing glare despite not being able to see his eyes behind the slits of his helmet.

His bad language improved now that she was awake, but his frustration seemed to vex him with each moment he remained trapped.

She winced as she pulled her legs into her chest and wrapped her arms around her knees, continuing to watch him make every possible effort to free himself. He was tall. Over a head taller than her. The armor had hidden what muscles lay beneath the metallic protection, now on display with the sleeves of his white tunic rolled up to his elbows. She couldn't gauge his age by his stature alone. But his voice… There was a mature quality to the deep undertones that made her think he might be at least twice her age of twenty-two.

Unable to stand watching him make a fool of himself for any longer, she called out, "There is a safety latch on the opposite side of the helmet near the neck."

The man paused before his fingers dropped the rock he held in favor of fumbling with the undented side of the helmet. After several tries, he successfully located the latch and took a deep breath when the two sides of the helmet parted.

Curiosity kept her attention grounded as he gingerly broke the two halves of the helmet apart and lifted it over his head.

Her heart caught.

Brown strands of hair clung to his forehead from the perspiration inside the helmet. Serious, brown eyebrows were drawn together, bringing attention to the beautiful olive-green eyes beneath them. His nose was straight, and his lips were curved in an attractive yet natural manner, lessening the severe note of his expression. Light scruff shadowed his jaw, giving him a rugged yet handsome look to his overall appearance.

The soldier wasn't twice her age at all. But likely only a few years her senior.

"What's your name?" she breathed, but inwardly cringed at how breathless and awe-struck she sounded.

Of course, she should have seen it coming. But he only grunted and tossed his helmet aside.

"I helped you with your helmet," she pointed out. "The least you owe me is your name."

"Oh, so *I* owe *you* now?" He kicked the helmet and it scraped against the ground before hitting the trunk of a tree and lying still.

Uh huh. Still sour.

But in her experience…the most wounded of men were generally the sourest of them all. What had happened to him to make him so…salty? Salty and sour. Not a great combination.

"You're hurt," she commented when she spotted the fresh trail of blood running from his ear and down his neck, joining a second river that was more of a red-brown color. An older wound.

"Just a scratch."

He abandoned his armor and began packing up the saddlebags before securing the saddle to the horse once more. His glare alone encouraged her to scramble out of the bedroll, which he rolled back up and fastened to the saddle next.

"Can you walk?"

She shook her head when putting any amount of weight on her foot sent of flood of agony through her leg. She braced herself against the nearby boulder and focused on breathing deeply until the pain passed.

"Nothing I haven't dealt with before," she said in a strained tone. But the look of confusion on his face caused her to backtrack to cover her mistake. He *must* believe her to be Princess Isobel. Otherwise, her life would be forfeit. "My footwear is designed to be fashionable. Not practical."

She held her breath, watching as he studied her with serious eyes that seemed to see right through her. Rather than commenting on her lie, he said, "I'm going to dump you in the next town and be on my way. I have somewhere I need to be."

Her lips thinned as she stared back at him. She hated to admit it, but she needed him. However, she hadn't any money to secure his interest, and she feared if someone learned who she was, the next ambush might be successful.

Knowing she would not last a day without him, she hardened her resolve while trying to relax her facial muscles to make her appear alluring and perhaps even desirable.

"I-I-I do not have the funds to pay you to escort me somewhere safer. B-b-but I will pay you in other ways."

The next face he made caused heat to climb her neck and settle as fire in her cheeks. A face of disgust. Of appall.

"I dislike you as much as I dislike any other woman. No, you will not warm my bed."

Embarrassment burned hotter in her face. "So…you like men."

The disgust grew into shock. "No, I didn't mean it like that." He took a deep breath and ran a hand over his face. "Is a princess so desperate that she will sell herself as such? Surely, all you need to do is flash your pretty eyes and someone will come running to your rescue."

Her lips twitched with humor, and some of the embarrassment eased from her face. "You think my eyes are pretty?"

He only scoffed and turned away. Rather than helping her toward the horse, he brought the horse to her. She couldn't help but notice he touched her hand and nothing else when he helped her into the saddle, as if the thought of laying his hands on her truly repulsed him.

She'd always been confident in her looks, but his disgust made her second guess herself.

Another frown pulled on her lips when she remembered she wore a face that wasn't hers. Her fingers lightly touched her cheek, the cheek of a princess that was years younger than what lay beneath the mask. The face that was probably ten years younger than himself.

No wonder he was disgusted. He likely thought her a child, barely on the cusp of womanhood.

"Then what do you want? You are strong enough to protect me. I need to get home."

"I was half paid to deliver you to your husband."

"He's *not* my husband." She huffed but her hands quickly clutched onto the pommel of the saddle as the horse rocked forward with its first step as the man led him by the bit. "Vows have not been spoken."

He turned slightly and eyed her over his shoulder. "For having known your maid most of your life, you do not seem shaken by her death."

Emmaline pulled her gaze away and stared into her lap, feigning sorrow. She had known the woman for only hours, and her death was rather unfortunate. But how could she mourn someone she didn't know?

However, she didn't have to feign her wariness. "Why did you save me if you despise me so?"

His head tilted downward, shadowing his expression from her view. "How could I not?"

Frustration clawed at her, at the way this man avoided her questions and deflected and changed the subject with well-practiced ease. She knew not a single thing about him besides his good looks and sour personality.

"All right, *Jack*," she said with a high level of feigned confidence. "Get me to this town and we'll go from there."

Surprisingly, his mouth twitched at the name, almost as if her attempt to guess it amused him.

"That's not my name."

"It is now. At least until you give me your real name. We are going to be stuck with each other for days, after all."

The mention brought the scowl out of his face right on time. "I believe the next town is only a day away. That's as far as I will take you."

"Because you are not enough of a beast to leave me here outside by myself."

"I can't be *seen* with you!" he hissed. But then his eyebrows shot up, and he turned forward quickly as if he hadn't meant to say the words. "I do not want to be responsible for you," he reiterated quietly.

She shook her head and clicked her tongue. "Sour Jack. No honor. No patience. No kindness. You are every woman's dream."

"You are just a girl."

Aaaannndd there it is.

Princess Isobel was seventeen years old. But Emmaline was twenty-two.

At the thought, her fingernails scratched at the edge of the well-hidden mask of makeup at the edge of her jaw. The mistaken identity was what might kill her. But at the moment, it was also saving her life. All she needed to do was rope this man into staying with her to ensure her survival.

She eyed the numerous weapons on his person from a bow to daggers to knives to a sword. She'd seen him use them, too. At least for a brief moment while she was getting attacked. Though, she hadn't realized he had been there to help her at the time.

Birdsong flitted overhead in the boughs, bellying the danger lurking behind them. Sunlight broke through the branches, almost tricking her into thinking they were safe and nothing terrible could touch them.

Her attention shifted to her foot draped over the side of the saddle. Pain rocked through her ankle with each step the horse took through the winding forest path. She'd broken her foot before in her line of work, and this didn't hurt nearly as much. But even a sprained ankle was dangerous if it forced her to rely on getting around some other way.

"Should you have left your armor behind?" she called to him when the silence lasted too long. "Someone might find it."

The man gestured behind him with a disgruntled expression. "If you'd like to carry it, be my guest."

With a *tsk* from her mouth and a shake of her head, she replied, "What will make Sour Jack sweeter?"

No response.

She tipped her head to the side and studied him again. For years, she had watched people and learned to recognize the intent and emotion behind every facial expression. But Jack was difficult to read. He was quiet. And she reckoned he preferred silence to conversation. His sourness indicated hurt or inner disdain. But she could never forget how he'd come to her rescue. How he'd fought without a care for himself to get to her side. His strong arms around her waist as he'd helped her onto the horse… The desperation in his firm hold to escape the enemy.

Jack hid his heart well. However, it was there. Just beyond reach but there just the same.

Although Emmaline didn't bode well with silence, she gave it to him, especially because he seemed to need it.

Even as the silence stretched for minutes. And then a half hour. An hour… The pain in her foot flared up until the agony became nearly unbearable. Her back ached from sitting so long in the saddle without reprieve, especially when she was not used to riding horses for long periods of time. And the dratted skirts. They tangled her legs, confining them in a way that made her suspect they were purposefully created to keep her from running.

"Can we stop?" she asked, doing her best to keep the fatigue from her voice. "Please, can we take a rest?"

The man glanced at her over his shoulder before nodding. He led the horse through the underbrush off to the side of the road, and with each passing minute, the sound of running water grew louder in her ears.

When she spotted the sunlight glinting off calm waters, she sighed in relief. What she wouldn't give to refresh herself for the next leg of the journey. She was almost surprised Sour Jack was allowing it.

They stopped next to a small stream rushing over fist-sized rocks, and immediately, the horse lowered its head to drink. Jack paid her no heed, not even to help her down from the creature. She landed wrong on her injured foot and cried out as a shooting pain climbed from her foot to her ankle to her leg.

Jack's head shot up, a flicker of concern flashing across his eyes before his expression fell into an emotionless mask once again. She tried hard to hold back another wince as she attempted to remain stoic in the man's presence. Thankfully, the injury wasn't enough to keep her down.

"I need privacy."

He glanced over her shoulder, then behind him, before he grabbed the horse's reins. He turned abruptly and began leading the horse away.

"But don't go far," she begged. She couldn't allow him to leave her stranded there. But he only lifted a hand to show he'd heard her.

The river seemed to sparkle beneath the remaining sunlight before dark gray clouds moved to block it overhead. A sprinkle of rain hit her nose and then her cheek as she stooped to wash her hands in the water.

Her face itched beneath the layers of makeup on her face, but she dared not give in to the temptation to wash it away. She needed it. If only for a little while longer.

She cupped water in her hands and drank. The cool water rushed down her parched throat. She glanced surreptitiously over her shoulder to make sure the soldier was nowhere within sight. But she didn't spot the white of his tunic or the brown of his trousers.

Carefully, she scooped more water into her hands, allowed it to settle, before peering at her reflection in the still surface. The small, distorted image gave her a decent view of her face. The thin mask to make her appear younger and the accompanying makeup was still intact, and her hair still lay in short, blonde ringlets around her face.

But the *pins*. They stabbed her and caused her scalp to itch. Not to mention the dress. It was a beautiful lavender in color with comfortable sleeves, separated by white fabric at the shoulders and elbows. But it confined her legs, not even giving her a full stride in which to walk. She preferred trousers and a blouse.

A giggle escaped her as she envisioned her traveling partner's scandalized expression should he catch her wearing men's clothing. Surely, it would be too much for him to endure.

One by one, she freed her scalp of the hairpins and set them aside on a nearby rock. When she pushed the last pin out, she shook her long, blonde hair free, and it fell around her shoulders in a mess of kinks and curls.

She wetted her hands and ran her fingers through the tangled strands, slowly freeing each snarl until her hair was wavy and damp rather than coiled with knots.

Pushing herself into a standing position, she next surveyed her layers upon layers of skirts. They were beautiful and likely cost a fortune. But she needed more room for her legs for a longer rather than dainty stride.

"Perhaps I can cut a slit in the skirts," she murmured to herself. "That way—"

Someone grabbed her from behind. She screamed before a rough hand promptly swallowed the sound. A scratchy beard pressed against her cheek, followed by cold metal against her throat.

"The king sends his regards," a rough voice said in her ear.

The blade cut into her throat faster than she managed to fight back. But before the weapon slit her entire neck, the man yelped and stumbled backward.

Emmaline cried out at the pain and pitched forward, crashing to her hands and knees on the sharp rocks and coarse dirt. Her hand flew to her neck, coming back bloodied.

She gasped as she spun around, only to find her soldier striking the enemy with a fist to the face. She scrambled backward, eyes wide as she watched him tackle the man to the ground. His eyes blazed with anger as he punched the man in the face again and again, finishing him off with a well-aimed strike to the throat.

The enemy choked on air, and with one last strike to his face, his head rolled to the side as he succumbed to unconsciousness. Or death. She wasn't sure, especially with the amount of blood running from the man's nose and mouth.

Jack quickly rushed to her side, pulled a handkerchief from his pocket, and pressed it against the side of her neck with one hand while supporting the back of her head with the other. His eyes hardened as he lifted the handkerchief for a moment before placing it firmly against her once more.

She couldn't help as she clutched onto him with stiff, terrified fingers. Shock coursed through her chilled blood as she stared up at him, their gazes locked.

She attempted to speak, but the words refused to come when her neck hurt far too much. Instead, she pleaded with her eyes. For what? She didn't know. To save her. To keep her safe. Perhaps to simply hold her.

"The dagger nicked something," he said in a quiet yet serious tone. "I'm going to find somewhere safe. I promise. I'll help you through this."

Rain spattered against her face as she stared up at him with a backdrop of bright gray skies behind him. The warmth from her body seeped into the ground, replaced by an unforgiving chill.

The light faded from the corners of her eyes. Darkness shrouded her vision like droplets of blood clouding clear water.

The last thing she was aware of was Jack picking her up and holding her close before her arm dropped limply to the side, and the world around her became dark.

Chapter Three

With limbs frozen from terror, Charles could hardly move.

He stared down at the bleeding woman in his arms, eyes wide as his mind took him back to the darkest of all days. Instead of holding the princess, he held another woman. She'd been soaked in blood, too. Unconscious. Utterly helpless.

Thunder struck the sky overhead, snapping him out of his daze just as the flash of a knife whipped toward him.

He jerked to the side. The knife flew past his shoulder and clattered to the ground behind him. A man charged out of the cover of the trees on near-silent feet with a sword drawn.

Charles ducked beneath the swing of a blade and spun around, smashing his foot against the enemy's knee in the right place to hear a resounding *crack!* Rather than losing control of his emotions in a stressful situation, the heat of battle focused his mind, allowing him to think with a clear head.

The man howled with pain and stumbled forward on one working leg. The pause was enough for Charles to act.

With the princess still in his arms, he shifted just enough to grab hold of the dagger strapped to his thigh and pulled it from its sheath. In an agile movement, most of his arm trapped beneath him, he angled the weapon to stab the other man in the side.

The enemy swung his sword at him. He jumped backward to dodge.

But then the momentum of the swing knocked the man off balance, giving Charles the chance to stab him one more time in the abdomen.

With a grunt, the man fell over face-first until he landed with a sickening splash in a puddle created by the rain.

He breathed heavily as he prodded the man with his foot. The man grunted. But then his heart gave a start when he spotted Leonian yellow beneath the man's vest. He took a startled step backward as he tried to piece the confusing puzzle that was the princess together.

Why would Leonia try to kill their princess? It made no sense. No sense at all.

He glanced up, and his stomach sank when he found an armored woman on horseback across the river, her face hidden behind a gold and silver helmet. She stared at him for a few moments before turning her mount and riding away.

An uneasy feeling lingered in his gut, but he didn't have the time to ponder who she was or what she wanted.

His attention returned to the princess, and his heart dropped to his stomach when he took in the paleness of her skin. Blood soaked the handkerchief he held to her neck. And the sight of blood weaved into the clothing of her bodice caused him to freeze once more.

His chest tightened. His breaths quickened. His mind panicked.

He couldn't lose her. He couldn't!

The ice that seemed to trap his legs in a cold, numbing web tried to stumble him as he rushed toward his horse. All he could recall was death and loss and devastation as he kicked the creature into a gallop while he held the woman close.

Rain drenched him down the front in his desperation to place distance between himself and the enemy, not knowing how many assassins had been sent to claim the princess's life. He urged his mount faster, only slowing down to round a corner in the bend of the path to prevent the animal from slipping in the mud.

He rode for what felt like hours, all while the princess's face became paler, the handkerchief soaked with blood until not even a speck of white remained.

The next town was nowhere in sight, especially with a curtain of rain blocking his view. So rather than searching for something he wasn't sure he could find, he led his horse off the road and onto the unbeaten path.

Stay with me, he silently begged.

And with a leap of faith, he let go of the reins.

Soft, wet leaves padded their path forward as he allowed the horse to take control. The creature diverted from the path he'd chosen and continued forward at a quicker pace than before. It snorted excitedly as if sniffing the air. And after a few minutes, his heart raced with relief when they broke through the trees, and he spotted a small, run-down cottage before them.

Carefully, he dismounted with the princess still in his arms and left the horse beneath an awning attached to the main structure to keep it out of the harsh elements.

His footsteps quickened as he approached the main door. He pounded his fist against the rotting wood, but rather than someone answering it, the door flew open on rusty hinges.

He wasted no time before entering, kicking the door closed behind him. No one was home, and he highly suspected no one had lived there in a long while with the amount of dust that had accumulated in their absence.

Frantically, he glanced around at the dusty decor. Two armchairs separated by a circular table beside the hearth. An old, speckled mirror sitting precariously on top of a vanity tipping heavily to one side on a broken leg. And then a cot in the corner of the room caught his eye.

He shoved pieces of broken wood off the rickety cot and placed the princess on top. Blood continued to leak profusely from the wound in her neck, and again, he froze at the sight of so much gore.

His pulse pounded in his ears. His hands shook.

But then he forced himself through the panic and the dread as he searched the area for a somewhat clean cloth to replace the one currently soaked through. The only dry fabric was…

He winced as he shoved the princess's outer skirts to her knees. "Sorry," he murmured before taking his dagger and slicing the inner skirt from the bottom. He quickly replaced the bloodied handkerchief with the new underskirt.

The slice was deep.

It needed stitches.

A heavy breath escaped him as he tried to focus his mind. In the heat of battle, his head was clear. But with a bloodied woman in front of him?

He didn't know what to do.

Another shaky breath left his lungs as he fought the darkness of his past and tried to concentrate on the present. His stepsister had once taught him how to sew on a button. Stitches couldn't be too different.

Leaving her for mere moments, he rushed back outside into the pouring rain and rummaged through the saddlebags. He managed to locate a sewing kit many soldiers kept with them in case a button worked its way loose. The Mother Goddess only knew why. More than half the soldiers likely didn't know how to work a needle. Himself included.

The princess didn't wake, even when he slammed the door closed behind him to block out the storm raging outside. He took out a single needle but dropped it when his shaking hands couldn't keep it pinched between his fingers. After a frustratingly long attempt to lodge it out of a divot in the floor, his fingers trembled as he tried to thread the needle. It took five tries before he finally managed the feat. And then he began the painstaking process of pushing the needle into bloody skin and pulling it back out.

I can't do this, he lamented to himself when his efforts looked terrible. And the *blood*. The metallic smell filled his nostrils with despair and hopelessness.

But he pushed through the awful execution and tied a knot at the end of the thread.

When the previous cloth was bloody again, he cut another swath and pressed it to her neck. A pulse still beat at her wrist, and he shifted his hand to her mouth to feel shallow breaths moving in and out of her lips.

He retracted his hand, only to spot flaking skin at the edge of her jaw next to flecks of blood. With his free hand, he attempted to wipe the blood away. He inhaled sharply when his fingernail snagged on the flaking skin. But it didn't feel like skin. It was…stretchy.

With furrowed brows, he managed to burrow his little finger beneath the odd stretchy substance. Only to find her actual skin beneath.

For the longest time, he stared at her as he tried to make sense of this new information. When he'd held her, her body was not one of a seventeen-year-old girl. At least, he was quite certain. Something wasn't right about her. He'd known it for a while now. And this only confirmed his suspicions.

However, if he were to find out what secrets she was hiding, he needed to keep her alive.

For hours, he stayed at her bedside with a cloth pressed to her neck as he attempted to staunch the bleeding. After an hour, the blood ceased, and he fell asleep, only to discover the bleeding had resumed.

He made sure to stay awake from then on until the bleeding stopped entirely, and only then did he slump exhaustedly against the side of the cot. But then his gaze caught on the red soaked into the woman's pretty lavender gown, and his stomach heaved at the sight. The darkness threatened to capsize on him once again, and to keep his mind busy to prevent it from happening, he leaped to his feet and threw the door open.

A rush of wind crashed into him. He fought through it as he glanced around the vicinity for supplies. He located a bucket of rainwater—well, his horse had located it first and must have been drinking from it—and he snatched it up. Beneath the awning where his mount took shelter, he found dry firewood stacked waist-high and tucked several pieces beneath one arm.

When he returned to the woman, he focused on breathing deeply through his mouth to prevent him from taking in the metallic scent of blood. He silently apologized again as he cut yet another strip of fabric from her underskirts and dunked it into the water. He cursed his trembling hands as he dabbed the blood from her bodice, trying to scrub the red out the best he could while making sure not to touch…anything.

It wasn't easy. The blood was everywhere.

After doing his best to wipe the blood away, he sat back on his heels and watched her to make sure she still breathed. She was unconscious and pale. But alive.

Despite his attempts to keep the darkness at bay, his mind flashed back to that night six years ago. The blood coating his hands as he'd held her dying body in his arms. The hot tears trailing down his face. The intense ache shattering the heart inside his chest.

And the silence that came from the certainty of death.

He dug deep within himself to find the anger and pulled it taut until his blood boiled with fury. The anger helped chase away the heartache and pain. Otherwise, he didn't know how to survive.

He reached inside his vest pocket, pulled out a small book, and tossed it onto the table next to the hearth. Next, he produced a small quill and bottle of ink as he slipped his next assignment from within the pages of the book. The piece of parchment contained coded numbers and letters, and he used them and the pages of the book to decipher the message for his next task.

However, his entire body froze as he stared back at his next assignment written decoded on the parchment. The two small words turned his blood to ice.

Kill her.

Chapter Four

The muffled sound of crackling reached Emmaline's ears as if they were plugged with cotton. A heavy weight seemed to sit on her chest, and as hard as she tried to open her eyes, she couldn't manage the simple feat.

She lay on something hard and scratchy, the darkness of her mind pulling her in and out of consciousness as she fought to stay above the surface of the ebony waters.

Something brushed against her cheek and then her head, followed by her neck.

Her expression contorted with pain as she winced, but hard as she tried, she still couldn't crack her eyes open.

She was vaguely aware of some time passing before her senses became clearer. Rather than a muffled sound, her ears picked up the familiar crackling of a fire nearby, the creaking of the rooftop following a fierce gale, and the soft flip of someone turning the page of a book.

The heaviness previously sitting on her chest dispersed to something far more manageable. And finally, after however long she'd spent in the darkness, she opened her eyes and blinked back the flickering light a fire cast on the ceiling overhead.

Turning her head to the side, she surveyed her surroundings. She lay on a cot within what appeared to be something between a small cottage and a large shack. The walls were a dreary brown, coated with dirt and charred wood. Water leaked from the rooftop and onto the damp, mildewy floor a few paces away. A table lay in pieces in the corner of the room, and one of the window shutters was crooked, though several sheets of paper were stuffed into the gap as if to keep the warmth inside.

Or to keep prying eyes out.

Her gaze shifted to the opposite side of the room where a rotted round table rested between two armchairs beside a hearth. Her heart quickened when she recognized Jack sitting in one of the chairs, his legs propped up on the table as he leisurely flipped through a book he held in his hands.

"Don't get up too quickly," he cautioned without glancing her way. "The bleeding stopped a while ago. But I reckon you'll be a bit dizzy for a time."

"What happened?" she croaked. But then she recalled the man grabbing her from behind. The knife pressed against her throat.

And like always, Jack didn't answer her question but deflected it with one of his own. "Tell me, princess. Why are so many people out to kill you?"

Her brows furrowed as she dizzily pushed herself to sitting, her legs draped over the side of the cot. "I don't understand."

He shut the book with a snap and tipped his head to the side until his gaze found hers in the dim light. "I'm still trying to piece together who attacked your convoy on the way to Amoria. But this time, I know for sure the most recent assassin was from Leonia." He shifted his body to gaze at her more fully. "Now, why would the Leonian king be interested in killing his own daughter?"

Emmaline's jaw clenched, but then she winced when the action pained her throat. Her fingers flew to her neck, only to find a bandage wrapped around the wound.

No, not a bandage. The fabric was lacy, as if it had come from…

She could have laughed at the way her legs felt freer with pieces of her underskirts missing, but she didn't dare when it pained her too much.

The man had saved her life. Twice. But she hardly knew a thing about him and therefore, couldn't trust him. She deflected with an accusation of her own. "I thought you were going to give me privacy at the river," she accused in a shaky tone. Despite her allegation, gratitude still leaked through her voice.

The man rolled his eyes. "Why in the kingdom's glory would I do that? People hide secrets behind the closed doors of privacy. I don't trust you."

Her heart sank to her toes. Though, the feeling of disappointment was silly, especially when she felt the same way about him, too. "Why?"

He didn't answer.

The shakiness of shock claimed her voice when she spoke again. "Why would you kill your peer? Did you not work with him?"

He didn't confirm the part about killing him, nor did he deny it. "If they attack me, they're the enemy. End of story."

Bracing herself against the corner of the cot, she grunted as she pulled herself to her feet. For a moment, her surroundings spun, and she clutched tightly to the cot as, little by little, her world stilled. She inhaled sharply as she took in the white shawl wrapped around her shoulders, one she was certain she hadn't been wearing earlier, nor did she recognize. Patches of blood stained the top of her bodice red, but it appeared as if it had been washed out because the fabric was soft. Not thick and matted with blood.

She eyed the man just as he eyed her. He'd taken care of her. Kept her alive. Treated her wound and made sure she stayed warm. Despite his act of nonchalance, he truly cared.

The man reached for the dagger resting on the table at his feet and fidgeted with the weapon, expertly handling the blade as if it were second nature. But then he slipped a piece of parchment out of the book he'd been reading, holding it inside his hand.

"I suggest you start talking. And quickly," he said as he twirled the weapon around his hand. "My employer gave me a rather…ominous…task."

He dropped the small piece of parchment on the table, which allowed her to read the two words scrawled across in black ink.

Kill her.

Breaths heaved from her lungs as she backed up against the wall, her heart pounding in her chest as he stalked toward her with his dagger in his hand. She'd seen how fast he could move. How expertly he handled a weapon. If she could not have him on her side, then she was as good as dead.

When he drew close enough, she grabbed onto his wrist. But instead of pushing him away, she guided the tip of his dagger to her heart.

"Just make it quick," she begged, a tear trailing down her cheek. "That's all I ask."

The coldness in the man's eyes chilled her bones. But then panic clawed at her when he retracted the weapon from over her heart and pulled on her hair to expose her neck. He placed the dagger against her throat, and each breath became more difficult in the face of her terror.

No! she shouted in her mind as she winced and closed her eyes. *This is not how I want to die.*

But he held the blade, and she knew she was completely powerless in his presence. If she must die, she wanted it to be as swift and painless as possible.

A whimper escaped her as she kept her eyes squeezed shut. The cold bite of the blade stung her neck, but not yet with pain. The man leaned closer until his breath caressed her ear with the faintest whisper.

"You are keeping secrets, *princess*. I suggest you start spilling them."

"Or what?" Her voice wavered in the face of his threat. "You will kill me?"

"I am no assassin."

He moved so quickly that she hardly registered the swipe of his blade against her jaw. She squeezed her eyes shut even tighter as she braced herself for a cruel and messy death. But when no pain accompanied the attack, her eyelids fluttered open, only to find him back in his chair, legs propped up on the table, while his intense gaze held her own.

She inhaled sharply as her hand flew to her jaw. The edges of her makeup mask lay tattered by his knife, but the blade hadn't cut the skin lying beneath.

"What's your *real* name?" he asked warily, never taking his eyes off her.

"You still have not given me yours. Why should I give you mine?" There was no sense in keeping her fake identity a secret. Not anymore. But real names were dangerous. Especially given to those she wasn't sure she could trust.

"It certainly depends on who is asking for it. Show me your true face. And I will consider giving you my name."

"Will you kill me?" she asked quietly, her gaze flitting to the paper sitting on the table between them. She didn't know who he worked for. Especially because a great number of people wanted her dead. As the princess and as her true self.

"Unless you draw a weapon on me, I have no reason to end your life. Nor do I wish to."

Taking a deep breath, Emmaline crossed the short space of the room and stood in front of a dusty mirror beside the cot. She winced at the sight of blood spattered across one side of her face. Her makeup was smeared on either side of her nose and beneath her eyes. And the thin layer of a mask to make her look more youthful was cut on her left side all the way up to her cheek.

Hours of creating the mask…wasted. But it would no longer serve her when the last person she needed it for knew of her deception.

Slowly, she reached up and peeled the mask from her face. The stretchy substance pulled on her skin in the most satisfying manner, managing to quell the itch rising on her own skin beneath.

When the substance lay in pieces on the table, she scooped up water from the bucket at her feet and scrubbed the remaining makeup away before patting her face dry with a cloth. She lifted her head and met the man's intrigued gaze in the mirror. He tipped his head to the side, studying her as he fiddled with his knife.

"Well…" he started slowly, still watching her closely. "I feel a bit better about our situation. You're not seventeen."

She shook her head. "I'm twenty-two."

"I'm twenty-seven."

A relieved breath escaped her. Finally, he'd told her something real about himself.

As she gathered her hair in her hands and braided the strands together, she turned away from the mirror, only to find his stare following her movements.

"Where is the real princess?" he asked.

Rather than answering him immediately, she finished tying off the braid with a ribbon and sat on a dingy red and blue-striped armchair, her legs tucked beneath her. "I do not care about revealing my secrets, Sir Soldier. But I do care about my own life. I will not reveal anything that will have the king of Leonia chasing after me."

Unfortunately, it seemed he had already sicced his men on her.

"I don't work for the Leonian king."

She narrowed her eyes at him, now trying to piece together the new information. If he didn't work for the king, then…who *was* his employer? "Amoria, then?"

"If that were the case, I would have escorted you straight to the castle to marry the aging monarch."

The same frustration she almost always felt in his presence rose within her. She was safe from his blade, yes. But for how long?

Holding her head higher with all the dignity she could muster when her neck ached and her head spun, she said, "Give me something real about you, and perhaps I will tell you my story."

"I prefer to keep my life private."

"Then it seems we're at an impasse." She lowered her gaze as she trailed the end of her long, blonde braid through her fingers. The exhaustion of the past several months weighed down on her, and she wished she could lie down and sleep. But she didn't dare lower her guard when *kill her* still lay on the table between them.

After several long moments of silence, the man broke through the stillness of the room with the sound of his deep voice. "I enjoy playing strategy games in my spare time. I like to challenge my mind in quiet ways."

Soft laughter escaped her mouth. "I wish I could claim I was good at such games. But my talents lie elsewhere."

She made the mistake of glancing up, and her stomach fluttered at the intensity of his gaze, the quiet confidence of his posture. He stared at her as if he were trying to solve a puzzle, putting pieces in place with what little information she gave him.

"What are your talents, then?"

Her fingers found her hair once more, giving her something to do other than return his curious stare. "I am a performer. I sing and dance and—"

"—steal people's faces."

She cut him a scathing glare. "Did you not think for one second that I am not here of my own volition?"

He tapped the flat end of his dagger against his palm before he leaned forward and rested his elbows on his knees. "I am thinking a lot of things. I wanted to give you the benefit of the doubt by assuming you are not a harlot seeking a position of power in the Amorian king's court by disguising yourself as the Leonian princess."

Emmaline gasped, her face flaming with heat. Words flailed on her tongue as she tried to form a response to his rude comments. But unfortunately, she understood how he'd come to that conclusion in the first place.

"I had nothing else of value to offer you," she defended herself instead.

"There are plenty more things. Such as names. Stories. Secrets."

What choice did she truly have? This man clearly still hadn't decided whether he was going to allow her to live. And she didn't think she would be able to escape fast enough to outrun him.

"I am a performer," she started again, her gaze drifting to the fire billowing in the hearth. Her neck ached far too much to hold her head up, so she rested it against the back of the chair. "But I suppose my story starts long before then."

Distress echoed within the chambers of her heart, but she'd faced her demons of the past and come out stronger than before. "I lived in a small village with my family, with numerous fields and farms and plenty of land. My job was to fetch water from the well." Her mind filled with bittersweet memories as she recalled her parents and her brother, younger by two years. "For years, the king wanted our land. But as a self-governing village, he was not our king, despite our borders touching."

The man sitting across from her tensed at the mention of "king," and he stopped fiddling with his knife.

Continuing, she said, "He was under treaty to not take our land by force." Her head dipped, and she stared at the weaving pattern of her dress. "The people who attacked our land were not his soldiers, but mercenaries. However, we all knew who sent them." Her eyes smarted at the memories, but she didn't cry. She'd cried all the tears possible over the incident. "They slaughtered so many people. My father fought back with a *pitchfork*. My mother ran with me and my brother. She didn't get far, as she was killed soon after."

The flames from the hearth almost seemed to reach out in an attempt to grab her with their destructive hands. There had been a lot of fire that day, too.

"What happened?" the man asked quietly, and she jumped at the sound of his voice, pulling her out of the horrid memories.

"I was only ten years old. But I ran with my little brother. We hid and we ran and we hid some more. Until we sought shelter beneath a wagon. Madame Gina found us. She clothed us, fed us, took us in. And we joined her traveling troupe."

"And this is where you acquired the talent for stealing faces?"

He seemed most intrigued by that bit of information, but she supposed it was the part that affected him the most.

She nodded, giving him a small grin. "I am very good at it."

"Clearly."

But then she sighed. "Good enough that the king of Leonia took notice. Two of his men snatched me after a show. They gagged me. Put a bag over my head. And next thing I knew, I was in the palace dungeon."

When she didn't elaborate, he leaned forward with eyebrows drawn. "Why would the king need you?"

Emmaline laughed wryly as she turned her attention to massaging the lingering pain in her foot. "The young princess was about to marry an old man. What do you think happened?"

"She ran away."

She nodded again, confirming his words. "It's much, much worse than that. She ran away to *get pregnant* so there would be no chance she would have to marry the old man and bear his children before his death. Her plight was successful. But the king's men found her, and the king secretly sent her to live at a monastery until after the child was born."

"He captured you to take her place."

A shiver ran down her spine as he spoke out loud what she hadn't wanted to say. "He threatened me with death. What else was I supposed to do but follow his orders at knifepoint?"

He leaned forward even more, putting him closer to where she rested her foot against the edge of the table. Despite herself, her will weakened when the intensity of his green gaze tied her stomach in knots. How could a man be so terrifying yet so alluring at the same time?

He asked, "Who tried to kill you as the princess?"

Shaking her head, she forcefully pulled her gaze away from him to allow her to focus. "I don't know. Perhaps someone who didn't want the alliance between kingdoms to happen."

"And will the Leonian king come after you again?"

A breath shuddered from her lungs. "I don't know."

The man stood, inspecting the windows, and tugging on the door as if to make sure it was locked. Surely, it wasn't meant to lock her in. But to lock everyone *out*. He was paranoid but careful, and she got the distinct sense he was no ordinary soldier.

"You never told me the name of the king who ran you out of your home."

She rubbed her hands up and down her arms as a relentless chill crawled up her body, so cold that even the warmth from the fire couldn't chase it away. "King Harold Avington of Armandy."

The man's face paled, his eyes far away as if he were somewhere other than the small room. His jaw clenched. His fists tightened until his knuckles turned white.

He grabbed the small piece of parchment on the table between them, crumpled it up, and tossed it into the flames. The edges of the paper caught fire, curling inward and turning black until nothing remained but cinders.

"I will take you back home," he vowed, sheathing his dagger next. "I swear to keep you safe from harm."

She nearly wept as the tension left her body, replaced by relief and gratitude. She was safe with him. She could feel it to the very bottom of her soul. "My name is Emmaline. Emma."

His expression softened as his gaze found her within the flickering shadows. Until now, he'd only looked at her with hardness and steel. But the way he looked at her now... With such tenderness in his eyes and understanding in his expression. There was something there other than cold detachment.

"My name is Charles."

Chapter Five

Why had he given her his real name?

A frown remained a permanent fixture on Charles' face the next day as he held his horse's reins loosely in one hand while allowing the creature to graze. He'd given Emmaline his real name. Well, the real name he'd gone by for the last six years of his life. He often gave people his fake names and fabricated backstories. But not a single thing he'd told her was false.

Like a flower drawn to sunlight, his attention shifted to the woman in question as she exited the cottage, leaning heavily on the makeshift cane he'd crafted for her during the wee hours of the night. Her foot was much improved after spending some time in bed, and her skin had transitioned from pale to a healthier coloring.

His gaze roamed over her unfamiliar face, the daylight giving him a better view than yesterday in the near-darkness of the cottage. She had delicate features on an oval-shaped face. Thin, blonde eyebrows. Small chin. Gentle, cobalt-blue eyes. Her lips were full and pink unlike the mask she wore earlier, which had given her thin, pale lips.

He much preferred her more natural face.

She was…

Pretty.

And older. No wonder she didn't have the body of a child. Or rather, a young woman. She was only five years younger than him instead of ten.

Her long, blonde braid swung over her shoulder as she lifted her face to the patch of sunlight breaking through the clouds and closed her eyes.

Turning his attention back to the horse, he patted the creature's neck and picked up each hoof to dig out the masses of mud collected beneath. He had no idea whose horse this was, but he imagined the owner was likely dead after the earlier slaughter.

Tension strung his shoulders tight as the *tap, tap, tap* of her cane moved slowly in his direction. He kept his gaze focused on his task rather than allowing himself to get ensnared by the blue intensity of her eyes.

After a moment, she spoke, "You didn't seem surprised to learn who I was. Or rather, who I was not."

He set the last hoof down and rounded the horse next to check for any cuts or other injuries, keeping one hand on the animal at all times to let him know where he was.

His mouth twitched with amusement as he lifted his head and gave her a knowing look. "You almost got killed twice. You spent a lot of time on horseback, and in the rain, at that. I shredded your underskirts to pieces with a knife. You injured your foot, and I know you've seen the botched job I did sewing your wound closed." He crossed his arms and lifted an eyebrow. "Through all that, you haven't complained once. It made me highly suspicious."

Her snort caught him off guard as she closed her eyes, threw her head back, and released unrestrained laughter. The sound was dainty and sweet but full of vigor and life.

But then she hissed, and her hand flew to her neck when the action must have pulled on her wound. She gave him a pained smile.

"I didn't realize you could make jokes."

Charles grunted and returned his attention to his mount. A small laceration lay on the creature's flank, but the horse was otherwise in good shape.

"Where am I taking you?" he asked as he saddled the horse, ready to get moving when he suspected the Leonian king might send more men after the fake princess. He heavily assumed the king wanted to permanently silence his not-daughter and keep her from spilling secrets, which was why he'd sent assassins to finish the job.

A scowl returned to his face. Kings. Tyrants. All of them. They killed and destroyed and never gave back more than they took.

"My troupe was in Leonia weeks ago. They were headed to Edilann next. But…" She rubbed a hand up and down her arm, her gaze far away. "I'm not sure if my brother would have left without me. They likely don't know what happened, why I've been absent for so long."

"The best way to follow a trail is to start from the beginning."

The woman nodded. "I know you have better things to do than escort an unpaying nobody across the kingdom."

True. But a detour wasn't going to hurt anyone. "You're not a nobody," he grunted, rounding the horse to place the bridle bit into its mouth. And to hide from the vulnerability in his words. "You're Emmaline. If you have a name, you're a somebody."

He frowned and forced a wall of cool detachment between them. Warming up to her just because they shared a tragic past wasn't something he was willing to allow. He grunted again before she could answer. "You will be a target in Leonia. Edilann will be safer. To get you across the border before the king's men find you."

"But I need to stay. I can't leave my brother behind."

Charles inhaled deeply and let the breath out slowly as he reached for patience. He shouldn't have offered to escort her home. But if he could prevent at least one unjust death by a king's hands…

Gesturing to her instead, he asked, "Can you change your face again? Maybe make your hair brown?"

"I don't have my makeup or tools." She ran her fingers over her braid, longing in her expression as if she didn't want to change the color of the blonde strands. "But if I come across something I can use, I'll do what I can."

Good, he remarked silently. *She's not vain enough to idiotically put herself in danger.*

Out loud, he asked, "How far do you think you can ride? We need to cover as much distance as possible."

"As far as I must."

He surveyed her up and down, wondering how he could have ever thought she was a princess from the start. Princesses didn't act the way she did, without complaint and ready to do what was necessary. Curses, even normal women wouldn't have acted so stoic with a slice across their neck and a long journey ahead of them.

Wordlessly, he helped her onto the horse's back and grabbed the reins, only for her to stop him with a hand on his shoulder.

He sucked in a breath and stared at the hand for a moment before he forced himself to step away. He shoved his emotions aside before he allowed himself to glance at her with an expressionless mask.

"We'll travel faster if you ride with me," she said. "Besides, you won't wear out as quickly."

"Walking is not going to tire me as greatly as you fear."

But then her lips thinned as her uncertain gaze settled on the saddle. "I am afraid I might pitch forward and fall off the horse."

Charles ran a hand over his jaw and held back a sigh. He didn't want to get close to a woman, physically or emotionally. He was already attracted to Emmaline. That was as far as he would allow himself to fall.

Still, her words held truth to them. She'd lost a lot of blood. She wasn't ready to travel. But she had no choice.

He grabbed the pommel of the saddle with one hand and swung up behind her, trying his best not to touch her. Even as he was forced to wrap his arms around either side of her to hold the reins.

With a kick of his feet, the horse started forward with rocky steps.

It only took a few moments before he sighed with exasperation as the woman began to talk.

"I'm not used to traveling by horse. Usually, I walk or drive a wagon." She hummed longingly. "I miss my troupe. They're my family. And there's just something about performing that makes me feel…alive."

He turned his head to the side as her words hit him harder than expected. He'd felt dead inside for six years. But… "I have a group of friends that have given breath to my life. I'm not sure what I'd do without them."

Stop sharing! he scolded himself and bit his cheek to keep from speaking more.

Emmaline turned slightly in the saddle to look back at him. "They sound wonderful. What about your family?"

"Dead to me," he snarled.

Her eyes flashed wide open, and suddenly, he regretted his harsh tone of voice. If only she'd experienced an unimaginable betrayal from her own flesh and blood, then perhaps she'd understand.

To keep her from inquiring further, he said, "Tell me about your troupe."

Thankfully, she needed no encouragement as she launched into the tales about her performing group. About Madame Gina who never forgot a face. About the misfits and outcasts she loved so much. And especially about her brother and how they performed together as "the twins," although they were two years apart. But no one in the audience needed to know the truth.

The woman had a set of lungs, even with an injured neck, he'd give her that. She talked for what felt like hours.

And surprisingly?

He latched onto every word.

A part of him craved connection and friendship. Another part of him wanted to shut it down in its tracks. He didn't need anyone.

With a frown, he realized that wasn't true. He needed people in his life. To love him. To care for him. To share laughter and friendship. But he didn't deserve it. Nothing he ever did would be good enough.

Which was why he was in the profession he was. He didn't have to think about people around the lies and facade. All he had to do was focus on the job.

"Oh, I do hope you will stay for at least one performance when we arrive," Emmaline sighed. "Promise me you will."

He gave her a noncommittal grunt before noting the color of the sky—a darkening gray-blue as the sun descended behind the horizon. They needed to find shelter for the night.

But after what happened the last time with the assassins…

Being on their own was no longer an option.

His attention darted to the dirt path they traveled, noting what appeared to be fresh tracks from a larger group. Hoof tracks. Wagon wheels. Footprints created from humans. He might have turned in another direction if not for the small footprints indicating that children had traveled the path recently.

The tracks led off the path and into smooshed foliage and broken branches. For a moment, his lips thinned as he contemplated taking this route. The group was easy to track, not hiding their whereabouts whatsoever. Their carelessness would put Emmaline and himself in danger.

But…

Hiding in a group was easier than hiding on their own. There would be more people to watch for unwanted visitors at night, more people on the lookout. And judging by the paleness of Emmaline's face and the dark circles under her wincing eyes, she needed a rest.

A safe place to rest her head.

He snatched her shawl where it had pooled in the space between them and wrapped it more securely around her, mostly to hide the blood stains on her dress. And then he led the horse on the beaten path, his fingers resting on one of the daggers strapped to his thigh.

As expected, he spotted a group camped up ahead.

"Whoa," Charles murmured to his mount, urging the creature to slow. He quickly counted heads. Eleven in all. Four were men. Three were women. Two girls. One boy. And a baby. The men didn't look like soldiers, but they wore hard, distrustful expressions as they spotted them down the road.

"Be on your guard," he said quietly to Emmaline.

She inhaled sharply as he dismounted and led the horse forward on foot. "What are you doing?"

"Making friends. Traveling in a group will put the soldiers off our scent."

"You can make friends?" she jested under her breath.

He scowled at her but didn't get the chance to retort when one of the men called out, "That's far enough!"

Charles stopped in his tracks and held his hands up in a show of peace. The way two of the men approached with weapons drawn unnerved him, but he forced himself to hold still rather than reach for one of his own weapons.

The two men stopped several paces away and eyed them with suspicion. The one with a bulky build, dark blond hair, and a beard spoke first. "State your business."

It was a good thing Emmaline's shawl hid much of her bloodied dress because they didn't need any more enemies.

For a moment, he eyed the group, trying to place their origin and social status from their appearances only. From their flowy skirts to the vests the men wore over different colored tunics, he guessed at least half of them hailed from Leonia.

Gesturing between himself and Emmaline, he said, "It's dangerous on these roads. My wife and I were hoping to find a larger group to travel with."

If his traveling companion was surprised at his lie, she didn't show it. Rather, her shoulders slumped a bit more as if to show just how tired she truly was.

"I don't see no rings."

Charles grimaced and stared bashfully at the ground as he switched his pronunciation from noble to peasant speak. "We're dirt poor, we are. Been savin' up for gold bands. Not easy in this economy." Hopefully they didn't notice just how many weapons he wore on his person. Weapons weren't cheap, after all.

The man's expression lightened, but the distrust remained. "How long you been married?"

"Goin' on two months." He forced himself through the wall of discomfort in his stomach and managed to lighten his expression as he reached for Emmaline's hand and held onto it. He hadn't held a woman's hand in, well, six years. "We're travelin' to visit family. Thought we'd be there already but took a wrong turn."

After a moment of casting suspicious glances at them, the man's wall of distrust broke entirely as he gestured them toward the others. "Yer welcome to join us for the night. But we're not sharin' food."

Charles nodded his thanks and followed the man into their camp, overly aware of the plentiful gazes staring them down. He introduced themselves to the others. "I'm Clyde, and this is m' wife, Lauren. We're grateful to stay with the lot of you for a bit."

He felt Emmaline's curious gaze on his back, but he didn't turn her way. Sometimes to protect oneself, you had to tell a few lies. He only hoped their presence wouldn't put any of them in danger.

After a few murmured greetings, he tied the horse to a low branch at the edge of the clearing and allowed the creature to graze.

Next, he reached for Emmaline, his breaths shaky as he placed his hands on either side of her waist and helped her down from the saddle. He lingered close for a moment to give the appearance of being a young, married couple in love.

What he hadn't anticipated was the shakiness of his breath. The erratic beat of his heart. The blue of her eyes to ensnare him as if he were a deer unable to move off the path of an oncoming carriage.

"Who are you?" Emmaline whispered, never breaking eye contact with him.

"Not someone you should get to know," he replied just as quietly and forced himself to take a step back.

"So sweet," a woman said, her voice making him jump. She held a baby in her arms, patting the infant's back. "Young lovers. I remember being in your place years ago."

Emmaline offered a smile to the woman while he took care of the horse and laid out the bedroll. "Our courtin' was short. But I knew he was the one for me."

Heat flamed in his face, and he turned his back to them as they continued their conversation. He shouldn't have been surprised at the ease in which she lied. She was a performer, after all. She lied for a living.

So do I…

In that way, the two of them were very similar.

"How did you two meet?" the woman asked.

Internally, Charles berated himself. If they were to keep up appearances, they should have gone through all the details before he'd thrown her to the wolves. No matter how small the assignment, details mattered.

"Oh, it was all rather romantic," Emmaline giggled. "He saw me all by my lonesome on the road and asked if I wanted a ride home on his horse."

Charles almost snorted. The story was vaguely true, but rather than ask for permission, he had forced her onto the horse.

Emmaline continued, "I should've said no to a stranger, but there was something 'bout his eyes that made me feel safe. I knew he truly wanted to help me." She cast a soft smile in his direction. "To take care of me."

Like before, his heart misbehaved at the sweet look she gave him, at the sincerity in her eyes.

I can't do this, he thought to himself as he hid behind the horse and brushed the creature down as he tried to regain control. Traveling with a beautiful woman was *not* a good idea. He'd known it from the start. But he couldn't just abandon her now.

Yes, I can.

She was safe with this group. He could leave her the horse and provisions and walk the rest of the way home by himself.

But his conscience wouldn't allow him to leave. He'd promised to see her home, and he intended to keep that promise.

"Oh, how sweet," the woman said, breaking him out of his troubling thoughts as he unpacked food to share with his "wife."

"He really is the sweetest."

Charles itched his neck, trying not to react to the comment with a glare or a scowl. At one point in his life, he'd been sweet. And *naive*. That part of him had died years ago.

He settled down on the bedroll and silently offered the jerky and nuts to Emmaline. After a moment, she joined him, legs folded neatly beneath her as she leaned close to him as they ate. Close but not touching. But their hands rested only a small space apart. Near enough for him to feel her energy caressing his fingers like a playful promise.

He snatched his hand away and stared into the growing flames in the middle of the camp while he ate. Emmaline made conversation with the others while he silently picked up information from the group. Who was related to whom. What everyone's names were. Where they were from and where they were going.

"You're rather quiet," one of the men commented across the camp, his gaze landing directly on Charles.

Beside him, Emmaline laughed. "Oh, he don't say much at home, neither. The brooding silent type, I like to call 'im."

Charles pursed his lips and narrowed his eyes at her. But when she leaned an elbow on his shoulder, his thoughts fled entirely. The heat of her arm seeped through his clothing and into his skin, causing a flush to climb his neck. His heart picked up a terrified, frantic rhythm, and he wanted to throw her arm off him and retreat to the safety of his solitude. But he couldn't do so without drawing unwanted attention and suspicion to himself.

The sky darkened further until everyone finished their meals and people began to retire to bed.

A hollow ache settled in his chest as he watched the young mother amble slowly about the camp, bouncing and rocking her baby. The infant's whimpers quieted, and its face relaxed as the rocking soothed it to sleep.

"Do you like children?" Emmaline whispered near his ear, and he jumped, startled at the sound of her voice.

He didn't answer. Rather, he tore his attention away from the infant and focused his energy on scanning the darkening area around them. The trees. The boughs. The hidden path. And then the people around him. Each were wrapped up in their own little families, speaking quietly to one another and tucking children into bed.

His gaze landed on the boy in the group, and his breath caught, his chest aching fiercely when he noted he looked approximately six years old.

Six.

It was the number he hated with his entire being.

Last year the number had been five.

"Charles," Emmaline murmured quietly, likely so the others couldn't hear her use his real name. "You're all right. Just breathe."

She rubbed a comforting hand across his back, and until then, he hadn't realized his breaths escaped as shallow gasps, his fingers clutched over the fabric of his shirt over his heart. His legs itched to run, desperate to escape the confinement of his mind. Which was why he surprised himself by turning toward Emmaline to seek the small amount of comfort she offered by resting his forehead on her shoulder.

"There you go," she said into his hair as his shaky breaths deepened, as he tried to block out the torment of his past.

The warmth of her arms and the soothing quality of her voice shocked him when it chased the darkness away. When it held the painful memories at bay and replaced it with a soft, warm light.

Emmaline began humming a sweet tune in his ear, pulling the darkness out of him one thread at a time until the drowsiness of sleep enticed him into the warmth the bedroll promised. Normally, he would have protested when Emmaline climbed in beside him. But he liked the warmth she offered and the soothing beauty of her voice.

He inhaled one last deep breath before succumbing to the fatigue of his body and mind and surrendering to the rapture of this woman's sweet, sweet melody.

Chapter Six

Emmaline's heart ached.

Not for herself. But for the man she lay beside in the darkness of a cold night, wrapped within the confines of a cozy bedroll. She ran her fingers through Charles' hair and continued to hum, as it smoothed out the creases of worry and heartache on his face.

His breaths deepened as if he'd fallen asleep, but she continued stroking his hair and humming a soft tune. In any normal circumstance, she knew he wouldn't have allowed her to touch him. But she hadn't missed the torment in his eyes as if he had been battling the inner demons of his mind.

What happened to you? she wondered.

All too often, she'd witnessed the glazed-over eyes, the nightmares, and the destructive pain of those who joined the troupe. Charles resembled one of those who struggled to continue forward after a terrible event.

Quiet. Withdrawn. Alone.

Her heart picked up, her pulse pounding in her ears as she moved her fingers through his brown locks from his temple to his neck, noting the faint curl beside his earlobe. She traced the outer shell of his ear, her fingertip brushing against the stubble on his cheek.

He was a handsome man. Handsome and mysterious and secretive.

But…she couldn't help herself from liking him. He'd saved her life. Twice. He was whip smart and skilled with weapons. Despite his earlier insistence to drop her off in the nearest town, he was making good on his promise to protect her as he escorted her home.

He was a good man.

A good but damaged man.

"You're too close," he grumbled in his sleep. "I don't like it."

Ah, there it is.

She almost laughed at the predictable way he tried to push her away even in slumber but settled for a grin as she stroked his hair until the worry lines smoothed from his face once again.

Little by little, her movement slowed until her hand dropped against his chest, her humming died down, and her eyelids drooped. And for the first time in weeks, she fell into a peaceful slumber void of fear and worry. With Charles, she was safe.

But then what felt like minutes later, she woke to birdsong in her ears, the bright light of morning, and small clinking sounds and whispered words as the rest of camp began to stir. A pleasant warmth rested against her back, which tried to lull her back to sleep.

Her eyes snapped wide open.

Her back rested against Charles' chest, one of his arms wrapped around her waist and tucking her flush against him inside the bedroll.

She dared not move.

She dared not breathe.

Heat climbed into her face at their unexpectedly intimate position, which traveled to the rest of her body until the bedroll became unbearably hot. Charles was *touching* her. Holding her. And she enjoyed it far more than she ought to, especially considering their short acquaintance and his prickly attitude.

All too suddenly, his breath hitched, and he stiffened against her. "Rat snot," he hissed.

Annnd it's gone.

He retracted his arm faster than she could blink and scrambled out of the bedroll, leaving a cold breeze in his wake. Perhaps any other person might have taken offense to the repulsion of intimacy in any form, but she tried her utmost not to laugh.

Unless he found another bedroll and soon, he was good and stuck with her.

"Can't get away fast enough?" one of the men laughed across camp.

"Uhh..." Charles' voice sounded sleepy and confused while she tried to feign sleep. "There was a spider."

Now Emmaline shrieked as she scrambled out of the bedroll, brushing herself off in a desperate attempt to relieve herself of the nasty creature. Everyone laughed at her expense, all except Charles who scratched his cheek as if he couldn't function through his obvious fluster.

Heaving breaths escaped her as she put distance between herself and the bedroll, all while trying to keep her shawl around her shoulders to hide the blood stains on her bodice. The others in the camp kept laughing, and she lifted her head, straightened her spine, and smoothed down her hair.

But it was too late. Her dignity was shredded.

His previous fluster forgotten, Charles raised an eyebrow. "A spider, sweeting?"

Her face burned. Perhaps from the fake name of endearment. Or perhaps from embarrassment. At this point, she wasn't sure. "Spiders bite." She challenged him right back with a stare. "You fled first from the spider, mind you. It must be terrifying."

It wasn't about the spider anymore, and she knew the moment he caught on when he narrowed his eyes at her. "Some spiders don't like enclosed spaces, especially when it puts them too close to another person."

"What is the person going to do?" she argued back. "Smash it? Not all people are unkind and unfeeling."

"The spider would likely disagree."

"Well, perhaps the little bug needs to throw out a net of trust once in a while."

His jaw clenched and unclenched. "This is not about the dame. It's about the spider."

Silence.

Emmaline glanced to the side, only to find everyone staring at them. A woman grimaced and glanced away. The baby's cries pierced the quiet of morning. One of the men coughed before continuing to pack his belongings. No one laughed anymore. No one smiled. Especially not Charles, who glowered at her despite their audience.

Her eyes suddenly became unfocused. Her ears rang. Black dots shrouded her vision. Weakness plagued her limbs. All too quickly, she couldn't hold herself upright and stumbled to the side, her arms reaching out to brace herself for the inevitable impact.

But rather than hitting solid earth, a pair of strong, familiar arms caught her. She tried to focus her gaze on Charles, but her head buzzed, and her surroundings spun.

A cacophony of voices blurred together as she fought for consciousness.

"What happened?"

"Give her some air."

"Water! Someone fetch water."

And then Charles' deep, soothing voice reverberated in her ear as he laid her on the ground. "Stay with me. Just breathe."

Her eyes smarted at the echo of words she'd told him last night, and without her consent, hot tears trailed out of the corners of her eyes and down her face. Especially when she realized she needed him. She needed Charles. To make everything all right again. To keep her safe. To keep her warm. She needed his comfort and his silent confidence and his prickly presence.

She didn't know how it was possible to need someone so ardently, but she did. Somehow, he'd wormed his way into her heart, and she found she cared for him more than she was comfortable with. Because caring meant an inevitable broken heart when he likely didn't feel the same way about her.

"I'm fine," she breathed, cracking her eyes open, only to shut them quickly when her surroundings blurred in her dizzy mind. "Just lightheaded."

"This is not fine," he growled moments before he placed a cold, damp cloth across her forehead. "You're not ready to travel."

"What choice do we have?"

He didn't answer, likely because he knew moving forward was the only way to stay alive.

As if overhearing their hushed conversation, one of the men they traveled with stated the obvious, "We can't wait for her to recover. We need to get moving."

"Have some compassion," one of the women argued. "Can you not see she is suffering?"

"Clyde," Emmaline begged, only wishing to use his real name. She didn't want to die. She knew it was selfish to rely on him so heavily, but she was sure if the king's men caught up to them, she would not be so lucky a third time.

"We're coming," Charles said while squeezing her hand. The small touch shocked her. He would never willingly hold her hand. Or at least, he'd made it clear in the past. "We'll take the rear. But we're coming."

The man said nothing more as Charles saddled the horse, packed the bedroll, and after everyone else made their way toward the road, he approached her with a look of determination on his face. However, she quickly shut her eyes when the world spun.

She couldn't go on.

But she must.

"Is now a good time to complain?" she jested feebly, and a part of her sparked with satisfaction when he released a breathy chuckle. It wasn't quite a laugh, and she'd still never seen the man smile. But it brought warmth to her heart, nonetheless.

"At this point, I will be surprised if you do." He hefted her into his arms with a solid strength, making the feat of mounting the horse seem effortless. "Don't try to stay upright," he ordered as he leaned her back against him and kept a steady arm around her waist. "You need to rest. You lost a lot of blood. Your body is still recuperating."

"Yessir," she murmured, turning her head to rest more fully against his chest. Being trapped against his muscular torso and the strength of his arms made her feel safer than she'd ever felt before. "Promise to not let me fall."

"I could never let that happen."

Emmaline's condition worsened.

Charles teetered on the edge of anger, panic, and hopeless worry as she flitted in and out of consciousness over the next several days of their journey. One minute, her skin was flushed with heat, and the next, she shivered uncontrollably as if losing so much blood still threatened to take her life.

Of course, traveling with the others in the group slowed him down. He likely could have reached a nearby inn by now if not for their slow pace. But if the choice was between risking her life by veering away from the safety of the group and remaining with the others, he chose to remain. Death was all but certain should they leave. At least with the others, he could keep Emmaline alive.

Even if some of those days she seemed barely responsive.

"Emma," he murmured, shaking her shoulder.

The campfire crackled behind him, and the low murmur of voices in conversation drowned out the quiet terror in his voice.

When she didn't respond from where she lay in the bedroll, he placed a hand against her forehead. It was hot. And as he checked the wound on her neck, a sickening dread filled him when he found it inflamed and infected. They had kept it dry and clean. But now he wondered if the weapon used to slice her had been tainted.

"Listen to me," he rasped, his gaze flitting across the paleness of her face and the long shadows her eyelashes cast across her cheeks. "You must make it. You have to survive. You still haven't performed for me. Or have you forgotten?"

She shifted in her unconscious state, and when her lips parted, nonsense mumbling escaped.

He knew she wasn't his responsibility. Perhaps he could leave and not look back, cleansing his conscience of her after returning to Edilann. But…

His heart snagged on a thorny branch of shock when he realized that somehow, he had grown to care for her. It was a terrible idea. One he should never have allowed to happen in the first place. But he had. And now he needed to save her.

Because he didn't want her to die.

He ran the back of his fingers over her cheek. To check the fever again. That's all it was. "You fight this," he snarled under his breath. "I'm going to leave and hopefully be back by morning."

With medicine. It was clear she might not make it through this infirmity without it.

He moved to stand but inhaled sharply when Emmaline's fingers clasped around his wrist. She didn't wake from her slumber, but it seemed as if her subconscious was asking him to stay.

"Not a chance," he whispered as he pulled his hand out of her grip and watched as it fell limply to her side.

His breaths became shallow as he stood over her, watching as she lay still and pale like in death. He clutched his shirt over his heart, his mind once again flashing back to a day filled with blood, loss, and death.

If he could prevent it from happening this time, he would.

He saddled and mounted his horse, and without looking back, he kicked the creature's flanks and sped off into the night.

Something awoke Emmaline from the deep heat of unconsciousness. The gentle touch of a hand. The soothing hum of a deep voice. And then she felt the top half of her body being lifted into a sitting position moments before something cold pressed against her lips.

"Drink this," Charles' familiar voice murmured.

Her mind felt hazy. Her body seemed disconnected from her soul. But she trusted him, and therefore, she did as he ordered and swallowed each painful sip of a bitter liquid. Only moments later, darkness pulled her back into sleep once more.

Only for her to wake in a mind and body unburdened by the previous intense heat.

She blinked her eyes open, squinting against the bright light of an early dawn. Although her mind felt groggy, she managed to sit up without her head spinning and her body threatening to fall backward.

At the foot of the bedroll, Charles spun around, and the moment their eyes locked, her stomach tumbled in a frenzied dance of excitement. Charles was a handsome man.

Should that have been her first thought after waking from a feverish slumber?

Perhaps not.

But the green of his eyes ensnared her, framed by beautiful, long lashes. His facial hair had grown a little longer, enough to shadow his face in more than just stubble.

She hardly knew concrete facts about this man. She hardly knew anything about his family or his past or even his present.

But one thing she did know…

This man…this near stranger…had stayed with her. Cared for her. Had shown a deep part of his heart and soul by remaining by her side even though she was not his responsibility.

And she couldn't stop the warmth from flooding her at the notion.

At least until an icy chill caused her heart to skip with dread when she spotted the small flecks of blood dotting his sleeve.

"What happened?" she demanded.

He turned his sleeve to hide the blood marring the white fabric. "It's nothing. I handled it."

"Charles."

With a sigh, his shoulders slumped, and he rubbed the obvious fatigue resting between his eyes with pinched fingers.

"Mercenaries. I believe they thought you were with me when I left camp to find medicine." He released a long, labored breath filled with exhaustion. "You have a lot of enemies, Emma."

She glanced over his shoulder to find the others in the camp packing up for the next leg of their journey, and although she received concerned stares, no one was near enough to have heard his use of her real name.

"I never meant to bring you into this. Forgive me, Charles."

He only grunted, but over the course of their acquaintance, she recognized the grunt as him brushing off the matter.

She attempted to stand, and to her delight, her ankle didn't hurt quite so much, but her head was still dizzy, and she careened to the side when the world seemed to tip violently to the left. Charles caught her by the elbow and stared down at her with an intense glower.

"So help me, Emma," he growled. "If you crack your head on a rock after all I've done for you, I will never forgive you."

She laughed and lightly smacked his chest. "Good morning to you, too."

But then she swallowed hard at realizing just how near he was. Near enough to catch his scent wafting off his skin and feel his thundering heartbeat against her palm.

He quickly stepped away, only touching her elbow as he guided her toward the horse to use to keep her balance.

"I'll pack up," he said gruffly without meeting her eye. But then he paused, his back facing her. "We'll ride together. Until you gain back some of your strength."

Emmaline watched his retreating back as he crossed the length of the camp to speak with one of the other men.

She recognized the heat of attraction pooling in her belly. But there was something else gathered there as well. A fondness. A stirring of warm feelings. And for a moment, her heart cracked. For all the men to catch feelings for, Charles was the least likely to return her affection. Feeling anything for him was a terrible idea.

But…she just couldn't stop her heart from blooming when in his presence. She liked him. Perhaps more than just like… And she didn't know what to do about it.

Chapter Seven

Charles swallowed the lump in his throat as he glanced down at the woman sleeping against him within the confines of his arms. Emotion struck him hard in the chest, his heart racing in a panicked rhythm. He was responsible for this woman. To keep her safe. To keep her alive. The heavy burden was almost too much to bear, and he wanted to put as much distance between them as possible.

Then why did his arms tighten around her? Why did he turn his cheek closer to her mouth to make sure she still breathed?

He glanced over his shoulder at the dirt road and the fields on either side. A few travelers had passed them going either direction. But so far, he'd found no threats, nothing suspicious or out of the ordinary.

Especially not the armored woman on horseback.

He didn't know who she was. Perhaps an assassin like the other two men? Or a mercenary like the one he'd fought after getting ambushed outside the small town now somewhere behind them? But then why had she simply stared at him rather than drawing a weapon?

Well, he supposed he *had* defeated her comrades in battle. Perhaps it had scared her off.

The others in their party began filing off to the side of the road until they reached the middle of one of the fields. He grimaced as he glanced up at the dark skies filled with gray clouds and rolling thunder. A storm would hit them soon, and judging by the others setting up their tents tonight, they knew it, too.

Unfortunately, he had no such means of protection for Emmaline and himself.

"We're here, sweeting," he murmured to get her to stir. The others were too far away to hear his words but…one never knew who was listening.

"Hmm?" she said in a croaking voice as she lifted her head. "How did we arrive so quickly?"

"You slept the entire way."

She sat up farther in the saddle and glanced at him with worry pinched around her mouth. "I apologize. You must be sore."

In truth, his back ached, and his arms burned. But he shook his head. "I'm fine. Besides, it looks like we're stopping early before the trail gets muddy."

Her worried gaze turned to the skies, and her lips pressed together, likely reaching the same conclusion he had. "It's going to be a miserable night."

"I'll figure something out. I'm not going to let you get rained on all night."

He winced. It almost sounded like he cared about her. That was *not* all right. He couldn't afford to care about her. Because he had to protect himself. Never again could he allow someone else to hurt him.

"We've enough canvas for the two of ya if we squish t'gether," one of the men called over to them. Charles started when he realized they were building a tent, one large enough for a good number of people to sleep under.

"You sure?" he asked.

The man nodded and gestured with his head for him to come help set it up. With no trees nearby in which to secure his horse, he ended up tying the reins to the back of his traveling companion's wagon before helping Emmaline down from the saddle.

He held her for a moment to ensure she was steady enough on her feet before he accepted one of the wooden poles and joined the men in setting up the tent as quickly as possible. As the minutes passed, the clouds traveled closer, and the thunder grew louder. The wind picked up around them, making the setup difficult. But the moment the canvas and poles remained steady, even in the rain, everyone filed inside and began setting up beds.

Poor Emmaline looked weak and exhausted the moment she sat on top of their bedroll, even after sleeping most of the day in his arms. He made haste in passing her their meager supper that was meant for a single soldier on the trail for two weeks rather than a couple fleeing for their lives.

"I will buy you a proper meal when we reach the nearest town," Charles promised, but then winced. He didn't care for her. He truly didn't!

"Oh, I don't know," she replied with a teasing smile. "I do enjoy nuts and jerky for every meal."

"It *is* rather practical, no?" His lips turned up in a grin. But when she didn't answer his jest, he glanced up to find her staring at his mouth.

His stomach turned with guilt. With regret. And instantly, his smile died. He didn't deserve to smile. To laugh. To enjoy the small happinesses life sometimes brought.

He picked at the nuts and frowned. It was too easy to let his guard down around Emmaline. He couldn't afford to get distracted. Especially not by a pretty face.

The young girl traveling with them sighed where she rested against her mother. "I wish you brought your fiddle, Papa. It's just not the same without music."

"I know," her father answered, roughing up her hair. "But I'll play again when we return home."

Without thought, Charles volunteered, "Lauren can sing."

His body froze with regret the moment the words escaped his mouth, especially when the others gasped and exclaimed and begged for her to sing for them. He glanced over at his "wife" and gave her an apologetic grimace. Although he'd never actually heard her sing, he knew she had a lovely humming voice and she'd claimed she could sing and dance.

But rather than giving him a scathing glare, her entire aura lit up, her eyes sparking excitedly. She waved the notion away with a hand. "Oh, I couldn't possibly."

"Please?" the girl begged. "I really really really want you to!"

Others echoed her pleading.

Emmaline sighed dramatically, clearly loving the attention, as she all too easily relented. "Just one song won't hurt."

He chuckled at her dramatics, which snapped her attention right back to his mouth. But this time, he couldn't bring himself to hide his smile. She was certainly a breath of fresh air when he previously choked on ashes.

Everyone quieted as Emmaline cleared her throat. The tension of anticipation filled the air, the raindrops on canvas a backdrop to the excitement of eager waiting.

Then she opened her mouth.

And began to sing.

Charles' breath hitched at the beautiful flow of her words, and he was quite aware of his dumbstruck expression when the sweetness of her voice washed over him as a gentle, lulling tide. His stomach dipped in the most pleasant way, and he found his attention fixated on her mouth, on the way it moved as she sang a folk song he thought he recognized hearing from another assignment in Leonia.

He listened in complete awe of her talent. With admiration for her voice, her beauty, and just for *her* in general. She wasn't just a ditzy woman with a pretty face. She was someone he enjoyed spending time with. Someone who regaled him with stories, with her thoughts, with her song.

He could easily imagine a life with her.

He quickly cut the thread on that thought. It couldn't happen. It never would.

When she finished the song, the entire tent burst into shouts and applause while Emmaline dipped her head graciously. He didn't clap along with the others, but he certainly appreciated the peace her music brought to his soul.

At least until one of the men startled him with a slap on his back. "You lucky dog," he laughed while the women chattered to one another in another conversation. "You get to hear that every day? I can see why you're so smitten with her."

His neck heated, and he wanted to protest his words, but doing so would give their ruse away.

He glanced toward Emmaline, but then his insides turned to ice, effectively chasing away all his previous warmth, as he noticed the baby she held in her arms.

From where she sat, Emmaline cooed at the infant, bouncing him effortlessly in her arms and making him laugh the purest, sweetest, most joyful sound.

Charles clutched his shirt over his heart. His pulse raced. His surroundings spun. His blood heated and cooled. Heated and cooled. And when he lost control of his even breathing, he stood abruptly and strode out of the tent into the dim evening and light rainfall.

What he needed was some air. A lot of it.

Over the days of their acquaintance, Emmaline had learned to read Charles' small telltale signs of distress. The man was capable. Strong. Confident. And she'd certainly learned she didn't want to be on the opposite end of his blade.

But he was broken and vulnerable.

And she couldn't just sit by and watch.

She handed the baby back to his mother and started to stand, but the woman reached out and stopped her with a hand on her arm.

"After what happened earlier, you really shouldn't be up yet."

Her gaze lingered on the tent exit where she last saw Charles. "We've been havin' a rough time of it. I need to see to him."

The other woman gave her a sympathetic pat on the shoulder. "The first year's always hard in a marriage. Gettin' used to each other an' all. Smoothin' out differences. Makin' a routine. But…" She squeezed her hand and leaned closer. "I can see how much he cares for you. You'll get there. I know it."

"And…what if we don't?" she dared to voice the fear plaguing her heart.

More than anything, she wanted to grow closer to Charles. Because she cared for him. Too much. But he refused to let her in.

"If you both put in the effort, then you will. I just know it."

Taking the woman's advice to heart, Emmaline stood on shaky legs, reaching out to the canvas of the tent to steady herself. She took a deep breath and braved the cold, rainy weather.

Rain and fog obscured the surrounding landscape, and she found it difficult to make out anything in the adverse weather. But then she saw him. He stood in the field with the fog as a backdrop to his silhouette. His back was to her, his head upturned to the sky.

Although she didn't know how, if she could take a fraction of his pain away, then she would.

And so, she started toward him.

Something light and soft touched Charles' hand.

He inhaled sharply, ready to jerk away when he turned abruptly to find Emmaline gazing up at him with a concerned, somber expression. He didn't have the heart to pull away from her. Not when he craved her kind, tender touch no matter how much he fought against the notion.

"What woman hurt you?" she asked quietly, just loud enough for him to hear it over the pattering rain.

"It wasn't a woman."

"Then who?"

He swallowed, contemplating whether he should remain silent or spill the heartache festering his mind. He found he wanted to tell her, if only to take some of the unimaginable pain off his chest. "My father."

"What did he do?"

He stared off in the distance and then turned back to her with a tortured expression. "He murdered my wife and unborn child." Her lips parted, her shock and horror staring back at him. "And my younger brother distracted me, took me away from her when she needed me most, so he could do it."

Her expression fell into melancholy sympathy. "Charles…I'm so sorry." Thunder rolled across the sky, filling the momentary silence of his admission. "How did you—"

"I cannot speak of it," he cut in with a raspy voice. "Not today. Please."

Not ever.

No one who knew of him as Charles was aware of the heavy burdens of the past he carried. He had never confided in anyone, and he surprised himself by speaking to Emmaline this much.

"Is this why you dislike me?" she asked in a small voice, the sound nearly drowned by the insistent wind.

Only then did he realize they still held hands, but he couldn't bring himself to let go. No matter how much he willed it. "Dislike you?" He shook his head and released a shuddering breath. "I can't stand the thought of being responsible for anyone but myself after what happened. I failed her. And I'm terrified of failing you. I…I…" He cleared his throat, reaching for anger hiding somewhere within him, but it was difficult to locate when for once, melancholy filled the void instead. "I don't deserve to be happy." There. He said it. "I don't deserve to laugh or to smile."

"Listen to me, Charles." She stroked the back of his hand in circles with her thumb. "You can't blame yourself for what happened. It was tragic, yes. But it wasn't your fault. You deserve to be happy. To laugh and smile and make a life for yourself that will bring you joy. I'm sure your wife would never have wanted to see you so miserable." She squeezed his fingers. "And there is no possible way you can fail me." She grimaced. "Unless you follow through with your employer's orders."

"I won't." He couldn't go into detail without explaining far more than he was comfortable with.

Emmaline glanced down at their hands and absently played with his fingers. "Are you a mercenary?"

He released a long breath. "No."

"I can't figure you out." She paused to glance up at him. "You can trust me, Charles."

Vulnerability tugged at him as he returned her sweet, thoughtful gaze. He wanted to confide in her. To lay his heart bare. But… "I can't have you hating me."

"How could I?"

Oh, you'd be surprised.

But he said nothing. Especially when the shock of wanting her to like him ran rampant through his body. The surprise struck the back of his head, seemingly out of nowhere. He'd guarded his heart so well. And still he found himself wanting—

No.

He could not have. He could not want. He'd denied himself every happiness for six years. And he would keep denying himself until the day he died. He must. It was what he deserved. But he wanted something more than the darkness he'd lived inside day in and day out.

An ache fell over his heart as he released her hand. He opened his mouth to say something. To say *anything*, but he didn't know how. He was torn in so many directions that it battered his soul.

"The children set you off," she commented thoughtfully.

He could do nothing but nod, confirming her observation. It wasn't easy to travel with this group, but they must. Because he needed to protect Emmaline.

"She was due any day," he finally managed in a raspy whisper. "The doctor got there too late. He couldn't save her or my son." He squeezed his eyes shut to block out the images. The pain. The heartache. The devastation. But even then, he couldn't stop himself from speaking. "He would have turned six a few days ago."

"Oh, Charles," she murmured, squeezing his arm. "I apologize for calling you Sour Jack. I…I didn't know what you were going through."

"No, no, no. I deserved it. I was rather…sour to you. I'm sorry." He shuffled his feet and stared at the ground before wiping rainwater from his forehead with his sleeve. A part of him wished it were tears. He'd been unable to cry for…a very long time. Unable to weep and to grieve amidst the strength of his hate. "This time of year is just difficult. But I had no right to be unkind to you."

"You've been more than kind and generous. I appreciate you. So much."

His heart leaped in surprise as he lifted his head to find a serious note in her expression. His pulse thrummed faster beneath his skin when she took a step toward him and then another. Her soft, gentle hand curved around his cheek. Her other hand rested on his bicep. For a moment, he couldn't move, couldn't breathe, as he watched her stand on the tips of her toes and bridge the gap between them.

And then she kissed him.

A mixture of shock, happiness, and panic exploded in his head. His legs became too numb to move, his mind overwhelmed as he tried to process the flash of emotions and physical sensations rearing their head within him. The soft feel of her lips on his. The gentle touch of her hand on his cheek. The light brush of her knee against his.

He willed his hands to move. For his fingers to capture her hair and for his mouth to respond. But he only managed to remain rooted to the spot when the barrage of his own emotions slammed into him.

All too suddenly, Emmaline broke the kiss and pulled away from him, avoiding his gaze. "That was bad timing. I'm sorry." She spun around and rushed toward the tent, not stopping even to look back at him.

"Emma, wait!" he called after her.

But she didn't stop and disappeared behind the flap of the tent. Too late, he realized he'd used her real name. He only hoped the rain had drowned out the sound of his voice.

A frustrated growl escaped him as he kicked a rock near his feet, watching as it skittered across wet grass and slimy mud. He didn't know what he was doing anymore. He was confused, and it was Emmaline's fault. Because when in her presence, he couldn't reach the anger he so desperately needed to survive. His mind calmed when she sang. His heart responded with warmth to her touch.

He'd built steep, infallible walls around himself in the past six years of his life, determined to become cold and aloof and alone.

Yes, he wanted her. And it confused him. Especially because she seemed to want him, too.

Would she still want him if she learned who he *really* was? What he *really* did for a living?

Telling her the truth meant risking losing her…friendship. Or whatever this was. And he treasured this connection to her despite how hard he tried to push it away.

No distractions, he attempted to remind himself as he stalked back toward the tent. *No mistakes. No excuses.*

He knew he needed to end this connection with her. To protect himself. To protect her. But he selfishly didn't want to.

And he didn't know what to make of it.

Chapter Eight

oward, Charles accused himself as he entered the tent, his gaze immediately searching for Emmaline. He found her with the little boy on her lap—an interesting tactic to likely keep him from venturing closer—while she conversed with a few of the ladies. She glanced at him but quickly looked away.

And he simply stood there, doing nothing.

Because he didn't know what to do.

He'd hardly even touched a woman in six years, terrified of growing too close to someone. It was too late with Emmaline.

He knew it. She knew it.

No, it's not too late.

But the thought of leaving her created a pit of anxiety in his stomach. If he left, she would die. Simple as that. She only had a fighting chance if they crossed the border to Edilann.

Swallowing the lump of emotion in his throat, he pushed past the panic, the heartache, the anxiety and unabashedly watched her with the child. The boy spoke animatedly about a bug he'd found earlier that day, Emmaline captivated by his tale. She listened with patience and conversed with the boy in an excited tone.

For a moment, he tried to imagine his own son should he have grown up to be six years old. In his mind, he held five little fingers, and in his other hand—

His heart gave a start when he imagined Emmaline on his other side, her smile bright and her hair glowing beneath the radiant sunlight.

The beautiful familial image dissolved like butter in a hot pan until a sense of loss hit him square in the chest. He couldn't be responsible for two more people, let alone one. He would fail them. Just like he'd failed Lillian and David.

But…could a fling work? Only a few days. No more.

A huff escaped his lips as he turned his attention away from her. He was a forever kind of man. He didn't do trysts or flings. Why couldn't he be more like his friend, Barnaby, before he'd met his wife? Then this wouldn't be so…terrifying.

However, one thing he knew was he liked to solve problems. And he didn't want awkwardness to be an issue when they were forced to endure close quarters.

"Come to bed, sweeting," he said just loud enough for the women to hear. He knew he should have called her Lauren around the others, but the name felt wrong on his tongue. He didn't like it.

Emmaline lifted her eyebrows high. "Depends. Are there spiders in there?"

"None that're afraid to get smooshed."

"What if they bite?"

He stuffed his hands into his pockets. His face heated as a bashful episode overcame him. The other women didn't glance their way, but he felt their attention on them all the same. "Perhaps they're in a cuddlier sorta mood."

She regarded him for several long moments, which only managed to coax his fluster from his fluttering heart to his heated neck to his warm ears. The two of them shouldn't cuddle at all. They shouldn't even touch in any way. But his mind was muddled, and his priorities shifted into nonsense. He suddenly felt like a young man again, not even come of age as he attempted to talk to a girl he fancied.

Finally, she held out her hands, and he released a relieved breath as he grasped them and pulled her steadily to her feet.

The heat searing his ears grew hotter when he felt several stares on his back as he led her to bed and helped her climb inside.

"I'm sorry," he murmured when he joined her beneath the warmth of the bedroll. "My clothes are damp."

"Mine are, too," she replied in an equal whisper.

With careful fingers, he pulled back the wrapping at her neck to check on how the wound was healing. The scar was red and inflamed, likely from the lacy material rubbing on it. But it was clean and no longer infected.

His heart pounded with her nearness, refusing to settle when she lingered close but still not touching. It was as if she truly was his wife, and they were too far apart. He didn't like it.

He warred with himself, an internal battle raging in his mind. He didn't deserve a second chance to do this courting thing right. To love and protect and serve and grow beside another person. Another selfish part of him didn't care.

And chastising himself as he did so, he gave into his selfish desire.

Charles' hand slipped from her wound dressing to her hair. His fingers lightly brushed the soft strands to her scalp as he gently pulled her closer and placed a lingering kiss to her forehead.

It was all he was ready for.

"Was that for appearances or because you wanted to do it?" her sweet voice asked with layers of uncertainty in its depths.

"Both."

But mostly the latter, especially because he didn't think anyone could see them from their vantage point, anyway.

The breath halted in his lungs when her fingers lightly brushed his jaw, trailed up his cheek, and her fingertip circled his upper cheekbone directly beneath his eye.

"I love the freckle you have right here."

Love...

Instead of panic, his mind felt...at peace. He should have bolted at the mere mention of the word. But the way it escaped from pretty pink lips in the form of a soft, pretty voice...

Her words from earlier echoed in his mind. *There is no possible way you can fail me.*

He slipped his arm around her waist and hid his face in her shoulder. She had so much faith in him. So much forgiveness and understanding. And perhaps, after all these years, his heart began to mend after allowing him to confide in another person.

Her hand rested on his chest between them, a pleasant warmth to soothe away the chill. "I thought you were jesting when you said you wanted to cuddle," she murmured.

He only grunted.

She laughed. And then pressed closer to him until he held her within the safety of his arms. Because he swore to keep her safe. Somehow, a woman who had started out as a stranger he'd resented managed to become someone he cared for immensely.

At that thought, he fell asleep with a smile on his face.

Over the next several days, their routine was much of the same. Eat a small meal before packing up and traveling some more. Stop a few times to take breaks, especially to rest or feed the children and animals. Camp out at night, only to do it all over again in the morning. Their pace was frustratingly slow, especially when Charles knew he could travel far faster with only himself to look after.

But they needed the safety in numbers. So far, Charles had found nothing overly suspicious, and they hadn't run into anyone he'd felt unsure about on the road.

Emmaline was making a quick recovery from her wounds, and rather than staying off her feet much of the time, she now walked around without a limp, without a cane, chatting the other women's ears off instead of his own.

Because things hadn't quite resolved between them.

The kiss…

He brushed a thumb along his bottom lip as he recalled the soft press of her mouth against his. The sweetness of her skin. The whisper of a breath on his cheek.

He lifted his head from where he sat beside the lake cleaning his catch of fish, easily finding her like it was the most natural thing to do. His expression softened as he watched her demonstrate her juggling talents as she tossed three rocks between her hands. A sly smirk lifted on one side of her lips moments before she kicked up a fourth rock from the ground in a seemingly impossible but agile motion.

Her captive audience cheered. He couldn't help but grin as he watched her mini performance.

And when she kicked up a fifth rock… The audience went wild.

His lips parted in surprise as he watched her finish off the act by catching each rock and dipping into a curtsy. He knew she could sing, and now juggle? What else could she do?

The gold of her hair caught his attention, and he couldn't help but admire the way the last rays of sunlight gave her a beautiful, glowing aura. And her smiling lips… They were alluring, holding his attention and refusing to release him.

He wanted to kiss her again.

For years, he'd fought against any temptation to get close to another woman, but he'd never felt the pull so strongly as he did with Emmaline. He felt the fluttering of excitement in his stomach as well as the dread of possible failure. Did he truly deserve to be happy again like Emmaline had said? Did he deserve a second chance at happiness? Was it worth pursuing?

But as his gaze followed her movements as she helped another woman set a pot of water to boil over the fire, he realized she was most certainly a woman he wanted to pursue.

He snorted quietly at the thought, trying to think of a time he'd pursued *any* woman. At least of his own volition. Every "romantic" relationship in his life had been arranged. To put up appearances. To strategically get his family what they wanted.

But what did *he* want for himself?

Emmaline.

Her name whispered through his mind and burned his heart with yearning. He'd known her for two weeks now, and his pull to her only seemed to grow stronger with each passing day.

"That's a mighty big fish," a young voice said, startling him out of his dazzled daze.

However, as his attention fixed on the six-year-old boy, Peter, now crouched beside him, his entire body froze. His blood turned cold. His heart pounded a dreadful rhythm in his chest.

Peter sidled closer, taking in the knife in Charles' hand and the fileted fish in the weaved basket. The boy said, "Papa says fishing is for older boys. But I want to learn some day."

The boy's wide, brown eyes stared into his own. Panic clawed at his chest, and he gripped the fabric of his shirt over his heart. Would he face this fear? The terror of his past? Or would he flee like the coward he was?

Emmaline murmured a profanity under her breath as she glanced up, only to find that Peter had slipped past her and now crouched beside Charles, staring him straight in the eye.

She held her skirts and picked up her pace as she rushed toward them in an attempt to pull the boy away. But then her steps froze as Charles reached for the boy.

He placed the handle of his knife into the much smaller hand and wrapped his larger fingers around it. Together, they filleted the remaining fish while Charles quietly instructed him on how to accomplish the deed. Peter's smile widened, his eyes shining with pride when they filled the basket with what would become dinner.

Peter threw his arms around Charles' neck before rushing in the opposite direction yelling, "Papa! Papa! I cut the fish! Charles helped me!"

A faint smile pulled up on Charles' lips, and the sight alone sent a flutter through her stomach, made worse when he lifted his gaze and met her eye.

Trying to ignore the nervous flutters in her belly, she approached, adopting a casual expression to hide the way he lit up her entire mood without even a word.

"You caught a lot." She nodded toward the basket as he stood from his crouch.

"I enjoy fishing." He scratched his jaw, the scruff having grown a little longer in their recent days on the road. "It's—"

"—quiet and peaceful," she finished for him with a knowing smile. "Just like your strategy games."

His mouth twitched as he nodded, handing the basket of raw fish to one of the other men to cook on hot rocks. "It must bore you. You don't seem like one to enjoy silence."

"You'd be surprised." She moved closer, only wishing to close the distance between them and throw her arms around him just as Peter had done. "I love a good dose of quiet and energetic liveliness. But do you know whose company you would enjoy immensely?" When he raised an eyebrow, she answered, "My brother also enjoys such games. Perhaps I might introduce you when we arrive at our destination."

He simply nodded, leaving her to connect the pieces of the aftermath of his silence. He didn't say much with words, but his actions and body language spoke mountains more than his mouth. And if she read him correctly… Perhaps he looked forward to the meeting as much as she hoped he did.

Uncertainty ran rampant through her as two of the women glanced their way from across the camp, speaking to each other in hushed tones while they wore suspicion in their expressions.

"They're watching," Emmaline murmured, taking another step closer to him. "I think one of the women is beginning to suspect that we…"

Her words trailed off, not knowing how, exactly, to bring up their pretend relationship. If the others learned of their deception, they would surely be cast out of the group, putting them in danger.

"Then I have not been playing my part well enough." He reached for her hand and weaved his fingers through hers, making her stomach lurch with nervous excitement.

She tipped her head upward to meet his eyes, not having to feign the adoration leaking from her entire expression. They had been on the road together for a while now, and she felt like she knew him like she might a friend. Of course, what she felt for him was a bit more than mere friendship. But…

She trusted him. She was comfortable with him. Although still quite a mystery, Charles was a good man.

A nervous pit formed in her stomach, and she wasn't sure if it stemmed from holding his hand or the thought of introducing him to her brother.

Both, she decided. Her brother was overly protective, and she feared it would break what fragile bridges had formed between Charles and herself.

The strength of Charles' hand guided her toward the fire where they cooked and ate the fish for supper, the two of them sitting side by side on a boulder with knees touching. A warm safety wrapped around her heart, and she hoped more than anything it wasn't just for show on his end.

After the group sang songs together around the fire as they clapped along and the children danced, her heart was so full to bursting with happiness, that she took a chance with Charles. It was small, and a part of her feared how he might react.

With his back turned as he conversed with one of the men, she bit her lip and dragged their bedroll a small distance away to isolate themselves from the group. She climbed in, wringing her hands as her heart beat wildly in her chest.

When he eventually noticed, she tried to ignore his soft, hesitant footsteps crunching against rocks and then grass as he approached, his silhouette dark with the bonfire behind him.

"Emma?" he whispered.

"Look at the sky," she murmured just as quietly, awe in her voice.

She glanced to the side to find him lifting his head to the heavens to gaze at the dark sky filled with beautiful sparkles of dazzling light. But her attention faltered when he exposed the strong lines of his jaw and the attractive muscles at his throat. Who would have known that beneath the helmet that had been stuck fast to his head the day they met was a handsome face that managed to make her heart flutter and her emotions snag.

He did not seem aware of what he did to her so easily as glancing up at the stars overhead.

"My mother used to show me the stars from the balcony of her room," he said quietly, swallowing once and then again.

Her limbs stiffened as she watched him lift a hand and pinch his fingers together as if he could pluck a star from the sky. After what he'd said about his terrible family all those days ago, he had not brought them up again since.

He settled on the bedroll beside her, hands braced behind him as he continued to stare up at the sky.

"She got sick," he said finally, his mouth downturned as he spoke the words. "But now knowing what my father did to *me*... I can't help but wonder if he did away with her, too, so he could remarry someone who could offer him more offspring."

"Charles..." she murmured, touching his hand to lend him the comfort he surely needed.

Surprisingly, he kept speaking of the matter. "I was the only child she produced. She struggled to keep children in the womb. I was young when she passed. Only seven years old. But I still remember her kindness. Her grace. How her motherly embraces made me feel like I could take on the world."

"I'm sure she would be proud of the man you have become."

He swallowed again, and his voice escaped as a raspy whisper. "How can you be so sure of that? My life is so…messy."

"Because I know she would be proud of what you have done for *me*."

Although he didn't expand on what, exactly, made his life so messy, he turned his gaze toward her, the same unreadable expression on his face he almost always wore. It was as if he were thinking. Pondering. Strategizing and planning.

A flash of light brought their attention to the skies in time to spot the falling star shooting across the dark canvas. She hurried to make a wish on the star, wishing for the danger to pass and for a chance to be with Charles. She wanted to see what could blossom between them. To find out where a relationship could lead.

He leaned on an elbow, and her heart squeezed as he gazed down at her with soft eyes and a tender expression. Never once had he looked at her in such a way, as if she were a star and he the awestruck dreamer staring up at the night sky.

"What did you wish for?" he murmured as if he didn't want to break the fragile stillness of the atmosphere.

"Wishes don't come true if you speak them aloud," she breathed. But unable to help herself, she asked, "What did you wish for?"

Slowly, he lifted his hand and trailed his finger lightly over her chin, her jaw, and brushed a thumb along her cheek. Her breath hitched when his finger whispered over her bottom lip, as light as a feather to make her question if she'd felt it at all or if it was just the energy pulsing between them.

"I don't believe in superstition." The back of his fingers rested on her jaw, and although he no longer explored her face with his hands, she felt his eyes doing the job just fine. Well enough to make it difficult to keep her hands to herself when all she wanted was to grab a fistful of his shirt and pull him down into a scalding kiss.

But she didn't know where she stood with him. And she didn't want to frighten him like she had when she'd last attempted to kiss him.

"Then what do you believe in?"

"Fate."

A shiver of a breath escaped her mouth as she held perfectly still, afraid any movement might scare him away like a doe fleeing from the hunter's arrow. "Do you believe we were fated to meet?"

He didn't respond. But the way his eyes searched hers led her to believe he was still looking for the answer.

"Fate is a heavy word," she whispered.

"It is."

To her disappointment, he rolled onto his back and stared at the sky overhead. But rather than stay silent like he might usually do, he spoke in a thoughtful tone. "I would like to see one of your performances. I cannot lie—I am terribly curious."

She laughed and dared to shift closer to him until their shoulders touched. "You have already heard me sing. How much more could be a mystery?"

Yet, she wore a small, secretive grin that he seemed to catch, as he shook his head and chuckled. "You pull a new talent out of your hat every time the group rests for the night.

I'm half-expecting you to breathe fire and pull swords out of your throat."

"That's not my expertise." She giggled as she thought about those in her family in the troupe who were capable of such daring feats. And then she gestured to her face. "My talents are with a makeup brush in my hand."

"*One* of your talents, I might add. I saw your juggling act."

"It's hardly a talent." She waved away the notion with her hand. "Everyone in the troupe can juggle."

"Stop downplaying your abilities." He poked her in the ribs this time. "I'm trying to pay you a compliment."

She poked him back, and then he proceeded to make her squirm and shriek with laughter as he tickled her sides. When she attempted to retaliate, he grabbed both her wrists and pinned them above her head.

The breath whooshed from her lungs when she suddenly found herself nose to nose with him. Her pulse thundered in her ears. Every place their bodies touched became unbearably warm. She held perfectly still. Waiting. Hoping. If there was a next move to be had, Charles needed to make it. If and when he was ready. She'd placed her piece on the board. Now he must place his own if they were to move forward with this game called courtship.

But rather than closing the remaining distance between them, he searched her eyes as if trying to find a long-elusive truth. He spoke in a hushed whisper. "Do you truly think I deserve happiness?"

"You deserve every happiness, Charles."

After a long moment filled with hopeful longing, he released her wrists and fell back onto the bedroll beside her.

He didn't reach for her again, but he also didn't retreat. She tried not to allow her disappointment to show.

"Do you know the constellations?" he asked.

She shook her head. "I'm afraid I have not had the chance to gain much education outside the world of the troupe."

He smiled at her, the weight of his burdens dissipating from his eyes. "Then allow me to introduce you to the world of the stars."

Chapter Nine

Charles gasped, shooting upright as panic rushed through his body. Despite only just waking, his mind was fully alert and attuned to the absolute silence surrounding him.

His breaths heaved in and out of his lungs. He glanced around the darkened area, a sense of dread spurring him out of the bedroll and onto his feet. Several others stirred at his breathy outburst, grumbling quietly at him to go back to sleep.

"What's happening?" Emmaline slurred, sitting up.

He didn't waste a moment as he pulled his boots on and strapped all his weapons onto his person. He thrust one of his daggers into Emmaline's hands and gazed fervently at her.

"Something doesn't feel right. I have to go." Ever since the terrible incident six years ago, he'd never ignored the sense of foreboding that came before a storm.

"No!" she gasped, clutching onto his arm. "Don't leave me here."

The terror in her eyes spoke when nothing more escaped her mouth. She was afraid. For him. Especially knowing what they faced.

"I'm sure as hell not taking you with me." He cradled her face in his hands. "I'll lead them away. And I'll return if it's safe."

"*If?*" she squeaked. "Don't go. I beg you."

But his mind was made up. "I'll leave the horse with you."

He strode away from the camp. She raced after him. But before she managed to grab onto his wrist, he jerked his arm away and hurried into the thick of the early morning fog. The appearance of dawn gave him enough light to see the way ahead. But the fog obscured what danger might lurk behind the thick, cloudy veil.

Mud puddles threatened to grab onto the bottom of his boots and cause him to slip. A deafening silence surrounded him on all sides. No birdsong. No cracking twigs. Not even a whisper of wind.

He refused to ignore the dread pounding a heavy rhythm inside his chest, the unease twisting his stomach into knots, the constriction of his lungs refusing him access to the air he desperately needed to survive what lay ahead.

But the thought of Emmaline lying in a pool of her own blood urged him forward. He tightened his grip on the hilt of his sword hanging from his belt as he crept forward through the trees.

A quiet breath escaped him as he stepped over a protruding branch in his path, keeping his ears peeled for any sound not belonging to the forest.

His foot slipped in a patch of mud.

He gasped.

And then caught himself on the trunk of a nearby tree, the rough bark scraping his palms.

For a long moment, he kept still, forcing himself to take small, even breaths to avoid being detected by whatever made his skin crawl and the hairs on the back of his neck stand up.

Had he made the right choice leaving Emmaline with the others? The men carried weapons, and they were no threat to the women.

But…

Something was wrong. He felt it in his gut.

A horse snorted behind him, giving him mere seconds' notice to leap to the side. A knife whizzed through the air beside his ear and embedded in the tree behind him.

He ripped his sword from its sheath and spun around, swiping at an oncoming knife aimed at his head. The small weapon flew into the bushes. He lifted his weapon for the next attack, but it didn't come.

Rather, several people on horseback tromped through the underbrush, quickly surrounding him. He spun around in quick circles, keeping his sword between him and the four enemies on horseback. He was only grateful Emmaline wasn't with him because this wasn't going to be pretty.

His mind focused as he honed in on the oncoming battle, taking in each of their weapons. Swords. Knives. Horses. One of the men wore a bow around his shoulders and a quiver at his back. But it wasn't drawn. Not yet.

"Well, well, well," a woman called out, and he struggled to single out where her voice originated from when the four continued to circle him. "I thought that was you. *Huntsman*."

Charles gritted his teeth and swiped at the leg of one of the leather-armored soldiers who ventured too close. The blade sliced the armor. The man hissed and reined his steed back. But they otherwise continued to circle him like wildcats on the hunt.

"You defeated two of my men more easily than the average soldier should. You gave yourself away."

Wickedly fast, Charles dropped his sword to the ground, pulled an arrow out of his quiver, nocked it, and let it loose. It struck one of the men through the gap of armor between his helmet and his shoulders, piercing his neck. He released a shocked gurgle before falling off his horse and crashing to the ground.

He reached for another arrow but froze when their marksman trained an arrow of his own on him.

He clenched his jaw, his gaze leaping back and forth between the three of them, one of them injured at the leg. Finally, they stopped circling him, their horses stomping with anticipation of a battle about to unfold.

"Who are you?" Charles growled when his gaze finally landed on the only woman in the group. With a start, he realized she was the same woman he'd seen at the river. She wore gold and silver armor, unlike her leather-clad companions. Her face looked familiar.

"It hasn't been *that* long, has it?" A grin pulled up on her mouth before she blew a strand of black hair out of her face. He inhaled sharply, remembering seeing the face only a year ago.

"Poisoner." He cursed, not knowing her by her real name but by her moniker. She was infamous for torturing her victims for information using specialized poisons. "You are supposed to be dead."

"Dead?" She laughed but never broke eye contact with him as if knowing the moment she glanced away, she put herself in danger. "The only way to keep a king from sending men after a spy is to die. You know how it is."

The woman dismounted, landing on the soft, damp earth with a squelch of her boots.

The only thing keeping him from reaching for a weapon was the man's arrow still pointing at him. "You're working for Leonia now?"

She shrugged, her thin lips pulling into a smirk. "I was working for him this entire time."

He narrowed his eyes at her. "You never struck me as the double-crosser type."

"Then you underestimated me."

He eyed the other two men awaiting orders from Poisoner. If he could just take one more of them down, preferably the archer, then he might escape with his life intact. "What do you want?"

"The girl." She smiled sweetly. "Where is she? I promise not to hurt her if you turn her over."

"Your men attacked her at the river." His gaze wavered, his lips pressing together as he feigned discomfort. "She didn't survive."

Poisoner laughed, clapping her hands together. "Oh, how you can lie. I've missed that about you." And then she nodded her head toward the man on the ground, lying in his own blood. "He can't vouch for his words now, but he mentioned he saw a certain little someone kissing a certain little somebody." She laughed again as he scowled. "Grown fond of her, have you?"

"It wasn't the same girl."

"No?" She raised a single brow high into the hairline of her dark hair. "You called her 'Emma.'"

Charles internally cursed his stupidity. Aliases existed for a reason. He'd put Emmaline's life in jeopardy by not adhering to the strict rules of a spy.

Not bothering to continue the charade, he said, "What do you want with her?"

The woman took a threatening step forward and casually drew her sword. He eyed the gleam of silver while continuing to watch the archer out of the corner of his eye. If he could get her close enough… The archer would likely slacken his bow to avoid hitting her.

"The face-changer knows too much. We'll offer her a choice. To continue on in Princess Isobel's place…or die."

"Not much of a choice, is there?"

"But then again…you know too much as well. I can't risk you getting the information back to your *employer*." She laughed, her eyes lighting up with glee. "Now…to kill you or drag your unconscious bag of bones back to the dungeon?"

Getting captured would be one of the worst experiences of his life. He'd rather die than allow her to inject him with her poisons.

"My *employer* would be very interested to know his former spy is alive and double crossed him." He edged toward her. "I'm not going anywhere. And I doubt you have the necessary skill to force me."

His goading words wiped the smile from her face. She raised her sword and charged toward him, putting her close enough to protect him from the archer. She swung her sword blindingly fast, and he barely managed to duck beneath the attack. Using the tip of his shoe, he kicked up his own weapon from the ground and snatched the handle out of the air, spinning around and smashing it into the armor at her arm.

Poisoner stumbled forward with the blow, and he followed to remain close. Blood ran down her arm, but the injury wasn't enough to deter her. The woman sprang back into action, the two of them trading blows in a deafening clang of metal and insults. At least on her end. He remained quiet through the ordeal, trying to figure out how to escape the situation.

He silently cursed when the injured man joined her in the fight, attacking him from both fronts. He spun and parried and blocked, breaths heaving from his lungs as he tried to keep up.

A part of him realized he was only faster than the others because he wore no armor. But he was in more danger of injury, too.

Desperation clung to him as he blocked the man's attack from behind and kicked him hard in his injured leg. The man cried out and dropped to his knees, giving Charles the brief opportunity to reach for a knife at his belt and send it flying toward the archer. The knife struck him in the chest. His arrow let loose and sliced through Charles' thigh.

He hissed at the stinging pain, but it was only a small wound compared to the one the other man received. Like his comrade, the man dropped from his horse and didn't get back up.

In his momentary distraction, his female assailant struck his weapon hard enough to send it flying from his hand. He gasped at the pain spreading through his fingers from the blow. He scrambled for his dagger, barely managing to withdraw it from the strap on his thigh, and blocked the woman's next attack.

The strength of her sword against his smaller weapon collapsed him to his knees. He cried out as the second blow disarmed him, and he wasn't quick enough to dodge her armored boot as she kicked him in the chest.

He landed hard on his back and cried out again when a sharp pain near his shoulder blade grasped onto his consciousness and throttled it. Had he been injured? Why did his back hurt so badly?

He scrambled for another knife in his belt but barely managed to graze the tip of the small weapon with his fingers before Poisoner stepped on his hand.

Charles inhaled sharply at the sudden terror of being trapped. He tried to lift his other hand, but agony ripped through his upper arm, making it impossible to lift.

Poisoner's face appeared above him, her lips curled in a snarl as she threw off her helmet and then her chest plate as if the weight of it proved too much. She held her sword in a killing-blow position. "Now look what you've done, Huntsman. You have angered me. I no longer have the patience to do this the enjoyable way."

Her grip tightened on the hilt of her sword. The blade stilled in preparation to strike. The hand on Charles' injured arm closed around a rock. But before he tried to smash it against her, the woman grunted.

The tip of a dagger protruded from her abdomen, blood soaking into the front of her tunic. Poisoner spun around with her sword, and a smaller, lithe form ducked beneath the attack and moved to stand protectively over him, bloodied dagger poised in front of her.

Charles gasped as his gaze rushed over the blonde curls of Emmaline's hair, the fierceness in her eyes, the protectiveness of her stance. His heart beat wildly in his chest, the rhythm pounding through his ears.

No one had ever come to his rescue before. Not even in his toughest scrapes. She was beautiful. Magnificent.

Everything.

And he found himself in complete awe as she stood over him, the first rays of morning light striking through her hair like molten gold. Gorgeous. Alluring. Captivating.

Her voice didn't waver as she spoke. "I'm the one you want. Leave this man alone, and I will come with you."

"No," he grunted, struggling to sit when his back screamed in agony.

Poisoner clutched her wound and backed up several steps, gasping breaths escaping her lips. She was injured. Charles could finish her off.

But as he pushed himself to his knees, a hiss slipped through clenched teeth. Something was wrong. He didn't know what.

"Onto the horse," Poisoner grunted, motioning with her head to one of the empty saddles. "Quickly now."

Charles finally found his feet, swaying back and forth when his world tilted to one side and then the other.

Emmaline took a single step forward. He made a grab for her but missed when lifting his arm ripped agony through his back.

Poisoner hefted her sword up, effectively gaining the advantage against the much smaller weapon Emmaline carried.

His nostrils flared with anger. He hadn't gotten Emmaline this far just to lose now. Even if all the odds were stacked against him, even if he might lose in the end, he swore to protect her to his very last breath—

A rock hit Poisoner squarely in the forehead. She stumbled backward, only for several more rocks to hit her. War cries echoed from within the forest, and a blur of movement attacked his senses when people rushed out of the trees with axes and slingshots, attacking the remaining two living enemies.

Charles took the moment to grab Emmaline and crush her against his chest, shielding her head within the safety of his arms to protect her from the rocks. He didn't know if the newcomers were friends or foes.

But the rocks never touched them. The assault was focused on the two enemies, who, rather than fighting back, mounted their horses and fled.

And when a second attack never came, he decided the others were friends.

He held Emmaline at arm's reach and searched her frantically for injuries. When he found none, anger welled within him. The anger of near loss. Of almost losing someone so precious to him that the thought stole the very air from his lungs.

"Why did you come after me?" he shouted as he struggled to stay on his feet.

"Because I care about you, and I can't leave you to fend for yourself!"

He took her by the shoulders and squeezed. "And I can't lose my wife again!"

Her lips parted. His eyes widened. He dropped his hands from her shoulders and stepped back. "That's not what I meant. We're not married. That's not—"

"Em!" someone cried behind them, and he turned to find a man rushing toward them through the trees.

Emmaline gasped. "Ollie!"

She abandoned him altogether as she picked up her skirts and rushed toward the blond-haired man. They met in a fierce embrace, and she giggled as he spun her around and planted a kiss on her cheek.

A scowl settled on Charles' face. Who was this nitwit? And how did he know Emmaline?

"I was so worried about you," the man said, smooshing her in another embrace. "No one knew what happened to you, but it wasn't like you to disappear without telling me where you're headed."

"Oh, Ollie." Her eyes sparkled with unshed tears. "I missed you so much."

Another embrace. It was all Charles could do to keep from stomping over there and tearing them apart. He tightened his fist, ready to clock the man in the jaw. If he so much as kissed her again, a brawl would break out between them.

"Oliver, this is Charles," Emmaline said in a breathy voice as she gestured to him. "Without him, I'd be dead twice over."

"Ah…" The man named Oliver finally turned to acknowledge him, looking him up and down with a sweeping glance. He reached out a hand, and Charles did his best not to glower as he took it. "You sweet on my sister? Or what?"

"Sister?" The tension whooshed out of his shoulders when he glanced back and forth between them. The same blue eyes. Blond hair. A similarly shaped mouth.

But before he managed to speak again, Oliver released his hand and fussed over Emmaline. "We've been out searching for you for weeks. The trail went cold in the capitol. The people weren't keen on our kind in the city, so we were forced to hunker down for a bit until we figured out what had happened to you."

Our kind? he silently questioned.

But then his heart gave a start when he really noticed the others around them. They stood at least two feet shorter than him, each carrying some sort of weapon from knives to axes to small bows.

Little people. Or dwarves, as he'd heard others call them. Seven of them.

Although Oliver certainly was much taller than the dwarves, but shorter than himself, he clearly grouped himself with the others.

One of the dwarves tossed a rock in the air and caught it. "I'm glad we got to send those assassin scum where they belong."

Emmaline's expression softened. "Oh, how I've missed you, Fox. I don't know what would have happened if you hadn't found us."

"We were watching the fight. Very impressed with your skills, master bladesman." Fox dipped his head in acknowledgement. "Didn't get involved until we saw Emma."

"Didn't know who the good guy was," another dwarf explained.

"We're only glad to find you unharmed." Oliver squeezed her arm before he nodded toward Charles. "I suppose I have your friend to thank—"

The man's words cut off as Charles stumbled to the side. One of the dwarves caught him, but the horrified look on his face led him to believe something wasn't quite right. That and the terrible agony racing through his shoulder blades.

"I'm fine," Charles said through gritted teeth.

But the smaller man turned him around, and everyone let out a collective gasp. Oliver swore. Emmaline broke into a sob.

"Did it get his heart?" someone asked.

"He wouldn't have lived this long if it had," another answered.

"Don't pull it out. He'll bleed to death."

"He must have landed on it, pushed it farther in."

Charles grumbled when Oliver led him to a boulder and forced him to sit. "Stop fussing. I'm fine."

Oliver smacked the back of his head, effectively silencing his grumbling. "You have a knife in your back, blockhead. It's not in a good place. You're covered in blood."

Only then did Charles feel the sticky substance clinging to his skin, which he'd previously thought was perspiration. As the focus and shock mellowed in his body, he felt the exact spot where the small blade pierced his back. He didn't care about the blade as much as he did about...

His eyebrows drew together as his gaze landed on Oliver. "Is there poison on it? Should be white or red. Maybe yellow."

One of the dwarves approached to his surprise, rather than Oliver. The man touched the tender skin around the wound with gentle hands before shaking his head. "No poison. But we need to get this taken care of immediately. Keeping it in poses the risk of it piercing your heart."

He took several deep, shaky breaths. But his nerves calmed a fraction when Emmaline crouched in front of him and grasped his forearms. He held tightly onto her arms in return.

"Bear is the best medic at home," she murmured. "You are in good hands."

"Are you hurt?" He looked her over again, still hardly believing she'd managed to take Poisoner by surprise with a stab from behind, and she'd come out of the situation unscathed.

He hissed, his breaths escaping faster when Bear touched his wound. But he did his best not to move, not wanting to make the situation worse.

She shook her head and held tighter to him, her grip effectively distracting him from the pain. "I'm uninjured." Her mouth turned downward into a frown. "If they had found us in the camp… Charles, you saved everyone's lives."

"By putting them in danger in the first place," he grunted.

The image of her standing over him, bathed in beautiful, glorious light while she fought for his life flashed through his memories. Unable to fight against the pull he felt toward her, he leaned forward and rested his forehead against hers while continuing to hold her arms tight.

"I'm going to do this slowly," Bear said behind him. "One…two…"

He pulled the knife out. Agony ripped through his shoulder. And he screamed.

Chapter Ten

The bellow of pain escaping Charles' mouth shattered Emmaline's heart. She held tightly onto his arms, trying to lend him comfort with her touch alone. But even then, his eyes glazed over, and his body slumped against her as if he found himself unable to hold up his own weight.

"You've got to stop getting yourself injured," she jested, squeezing his arms as Skippy cut the man's shirt off with a knife.

"Me?" he slurred. "I think you have the two of us mixed up."

She tried to laugh but it escaped more like a sob.

He squeezed *her* arms this time. "That feels so much better with the knife out. Don't you worry about me."

"I'm not worried at all," she lied, knowing he instantly saw through her when his lips pressed together in a near-scowl. She opened her mouth to protest further, but the words caught in her throat when the remainder of Charles' shirt fell away to reveal his bare torso.

His bare, *muscular* torso.

Her mouth dried as her gaze roamed over the grooves in his abdomen, the strong muscles of his chest, the sturdy strength of his shoulders. His arms flexed where they continued to hold onto her, and for a moment, she forgot how to breathe as she couldn't help but stare. It was any wonder he was fast and agile, skilled and strong. He was fit. And far more handsome than he had any right to be.

"All right, time for you to see to the horses," Oliver growled, forcing her to her feet and prodding her toward the grazing animals. "Just steer clear of the back. There's a couple of dead bodies."

Her stomach churned at the thought. How many men had Charles been forced to protect her from? He was getting his hands bloodied, and it was her fault. She'd never wanted to put him in such a position.

Surreptitiously, she glanced over her shoulder at the man in question, watching as Oliver handed him one of his own spare shirts from his pack. Charles lifted his head and met her gaze, the side of his mouth twitching in what she could only describe as a coy grin. At least, coy for him.

But the moment her brother noticed her wavering attention, he glowered and motioned for her to turn around.

Something had changed between her and Charles. Something kinder, sweeter, and perhaps a little romantic. She didn't know when it had happened, when he'd softened toward her. She only knew her heart was falling, and it was too late to stop it.

Her ears perked up when Oliver started asking questions. "Who were those people?"

Charles cleared his throat. "They worked for the Leonian king. He wants to either take Emma or kill her to keep her silent."

"Silent? Over what?"

Emmaline released a long, exhausted sigh. "I suppose I have a lot to tell you."

After Bear finished sewing Charles' wound closed, the infuriating man insisted she ride the horse next to Oliver and his mount while he and the others walked. They decided to leave their previous traveling companions behind without a goodbye. It was safer that way. And then she explained the situation as best she could as they traveled, and Charles filled in the gaps.

Speaking it out loud exhausted her. She'd been away from home for too long. Running. Fleeing. Always watching over her shoulder. All she wanted was to go home and sleep somewhere familiar and seek comfort from her family.

"Shouldn't be too hard to hide you if they come lookin'," her brother said beside her. "A wig should probably fix the issue for a time. Plus, costumes and makeup. They'd have to burn our home to the ground before I'd let them take you again."

The reassurance of his words erased much of the anxiety swirling within her mind. She didn't know if the female assassin had survived after being stabbed, but it was sure to deter them for a while.

At least, she hoped.

Oliver pulled back on his horse to distance himself from the group, and she followed suit, dreading the inevitable conversation and the unaddressed complication.

Charles...

"Who is he?" her brother quietly asked, immediately jumping to the topic while nodding toward Charles.

"A soldier who saved my life."

Oliver raised an eyebrow. "You don't sound too sure."

She shrugged, her mouth quirking to the side. "He won't tell me. He has only confirmed he's not a mercenary or an assassin."

Leaning back in his saddle, Oliver turned his attention to Charles where he walked between two of her friends up ahead. Cub was attempting to make conversation, and to her surprise, the other man took the bait. At least a little bite.

"Something isn't right about him."

"What do you mean?"

His expression became pinched and troubled, his gaze never wavering from Charles' back. "I saw the whole fight, Em. They talked a lot, though I couldn't hear what was said. I think he knows that woman you stabbed."

Cold dread tightened in her gut as she recalled the woman's eyes lacking empathy and her ruthless attempts at bloodshed. "Why wouldn't he have said anything then?"

"He's hiding something. He's gotta be." He continued to stare relentlessly at the other man as if trying to figure out a riddle. "He fights really well. And the way he talks..."

"How does he talk?"

"He tries to hide it. But it slips through." Finally, he tore his gaze away from Charles and fixed his attention on her. "He has an accent. From *Armandy*."

Her fingers froze over the reins. The simple mention of the country's name burned holes of heartache into her chest. The Armandy king was responsible for the death of her parents and her friends. He'd taken everything from her. Absolutely everything except Oliver.

But then the warmth of rationale melted the frozen fear and uncertainty within her. "That means nothing. Plenty of good people are from Armandy. Perhaps he fled just like we did."

Still, Oliver shook his head. "Why the secrets then? Why not outright speak the truth? The man clearly fancies you. Why keep you in the dark?"

Heat flushed through her cheeks as she tucked a strand of hair behind her ear, her gaze darting toward Charles. "Do you really think he fancies me?"

Oliver's eyebrows drew together as he glowered at her. "You don't even know him. It would be best to stay away."

"What do you think I'm going to do? Run off with him?"

"Yes! That's exactly what I think you're going to do."

His outburst grabbed Charles' attention, and he glanced at them over his shoulder. Emmaline's heart pounded when his gaze lingered on her a little longer than her brother. Was Oliver right? Did Charles have feelings for her?

She lowered her voice. "Just like how you ran off with Quinn two years ago? How did you put it? It was 'in the name of love?'"

"That doesn't count," he grumbled. "It was rather poetic at the time."

Rather than goading her brother some more, she frowned at the way Charles hunched one of his shoulders, clearly injured despite his insistence that it barely hurt. Guilt punched her in the gut, stealing the breath from her lungs. She'd insisted for him to escort her back home. His injury was her fault.

She kicked her horse's flanks, and the creature trotted forward until she sidled up to Charles. "I've grown weary of riding. We can trade places."

The man snorted. *Snorted!*

"You fainted not even two weeks ago. Don't even think about stepping foot on the ground. Otherwise, I'll hog tie you to the saddle."

Behind them, Oliver laughed and slapped his knee. "All right, I think I changed my mind about you. You're not so bad."

On any normal day, she might have scoffed at them. But she bit her lip instead, tipping her head to the side as she listened to the two of them converse. She never would have picked it out on her own but...

Charles *did* have an accent. Not a consistent accent, but a few words slipped here and there as if he were consciously trying to conceal it.

What secrets are you hiding?

Oliver leaned forward in his saddle, a friendly, easy grin on his face but a calculating look in his eye. "Where you from, stranger?"

The man's answer was quick and gruff, full of surety and not a flicker of hesitance. "Edilann."

With his back turned, she and Oliver exchanged glances. Why didn't Charles tell the truth?

"Well, *we're* from Armandy," her brother continued. "Not a happy story there, but I'm sure my sister opened up to you about our terrible past."

"Mmmhmm." Charles said nothing more, closing off before her eyes and once more becoming the uncrackable wall she'd first met weeks ago. Cold. Aloof. Detached.

With lips pressed together, Oliver reined back again and shook his head, whispering, "Until he tells us the truth, I don't want you courting him."

Her nostrils flared. "That's not your decision to make."

"No, but he's a dangerous man. You are more sensible than this, Emma. You know nothing about him."

Her voice cracked, "I know his heart."

He frowned and pulled his attention away from her and back to Charles, whose shoulders were now rigid as if he could barely stand the pain. Skippy, ever the chatty dwarf, spoke loudly and fast enough to mask their hushed conversation.

"Sometimes, that's just not enough."

Life had been simpler when Charles hadn't needed to gain the favor of someone Emmaline loved and respected, and he hadn't realized he wanted to attempt the feat until the thought of living life without her broke off a piece of his soul.

"I don't want you courting him."

He frowned as he recalled the siblings' hushed conversation. Unfortunately for them, the wind had been blowing *toward* him rather than away, which had carried their voices in his direction. That, and he'd trained for years in the art of stealth and picking up conversations he was not meant to hear.

They knew he was lying about his origins. He didn't know how they'd found out. But then again, he could imagine the two had more street smarts than he realized, especially considering their occupation and their past.

He released a long breath but then winced at the agony racing through his back. He'd been stabbed before. In the leg. And again in the shoulder. But never in the back. He didn't even know how it had happened.

Surreptitiously, he glanced to the side to find the dwarves—Bear, Cub, Fox, Skippy, Gloomy, Hungry, and Shorts—chopping logs to use for seating and setting up makeshift tables around the small camp. He suspected they weren't actually their real names, but he was also afraid to ask.

A sigh escaped him as he watched brother and sister speak in low tones to one another beside the two horses as if they were arguing. Probably about him if he had to take a guess.

If he wanted Emmaline in his life, he needed to come clean. About everything. Perhaps not all at once, but a few things he needed to straighten out.

Smoothing down his borrowed forest-green tunic, he approached the two with caution. They ceased their furious whispering. Oliver crossed his arms and planted his feet as if readying himself for a fight. The glower in his eyes was enough to make him want to bolt. And the distress in Emmaline's expression… The hesitancy to trust him…

He swallowed his uncertainty and dropped his Edilann accent in favor of his native speech. "I don't like speaking in my native accent." Their eyes widened in identical blue spheres, and for a moment, he understood why they performed as "the twins" when they really could have been born on the same day. "I hate everything about Armandy. I may have been born there, but my true home is Edilann." He switched back to his Edilann accent, the one he preferred over the other. "I did not mean to deceive either of you. The memories are…too difficult. This is who I am and who I want to be. I want to leave that life behind. I hope this doesn't mean you can't trust me."

Oh, he had plenty more secrets, but was Oliver trustworthy? Were the dwarves? Was he ready to dig through the mud of his past?

Oliver stepped closer and raised an eyebrow. "How many accents can you imitate?"

He shrugged his good shoulder. "A few."

"And do you speak any other languages?"

His mouth twitched as he stared down at his feet, trying not to smile. "A few."

"Where did you learn them?"

And just like that, his good mood vanished. "Expensive tutors."

"Leave him alone," Emmaline murmured, and when her fingers lightly touched his elbow, his heart responded with a quick rhythm and unbearable warmth. "It's been a long day. He doesn't need you questioning him."

Although Oliver's defenses visibly fell, a new determined look shone in his eyes. "I think a little card game is in order." He gestured toward one of the empty tables the dwarves had set up. "Humor me, Charles."

"Ollie," Emmaline said in a strained tone. "Don't do this."

"I shall and I will."

Charles slowly lowered himself on one of the logs to prevent himself from pulling on his wound. Confusion drew his brows together as Oliver pulled out a pack of cards and a pair of dice from his pocket. Judging by the competitive look in the man's eye…he got the distinct impression that this was no ordinary game.

Chapter Eleven

Emmaline kept stealing glances at Charles and her brother sitting at the makeshift table away from the others. Each sat on a chopped upright log with a game of cards and dice between them on the table. It was almost comical the way they both wore serious, thoughtful expressions as they played.

Until now, she hadn't realized just how similar the two were. In temperament. In hobbies. Although Charles was a bit more serious and intense than her brother.

"Do you reckon he'll win?" Fox asked.

She laughed quietly and shook her head. "No one ever wins against my brother. He's too good, and Charles just learned the game."

Fox waggled his eyebrows. "But you want him to win, eh?"

A pleasant heat filled her cheeks as she watched as Charles stared at the cards on the table. She could see his mind working rapidly through the intensity of his eyes, even though he remained still and quiet.

"Oh, I know exactly what Ollie is doing," she said in a quieter tone.

For years, Oliver had told her no one could have her hand unless they could beat him at his own game. Poor Charles didn't even know what the stakes were. Even then, the wind was not blowing in their favor.

"He's going to have to try at least a dozen more times if he wants to have a chance at putting a ring on my finger," she laughed through her smarting eyes in an attempt to hide her emotions.

But her friend saw past it and wagged a finger at her. "You love him."

"I shouldn't."

"But you do."

"It hasn't been long enough. I couldn't."

But then she recalled the absolute horror of him leaving her behind, terrified she'd never see him again. She'd gone after him, only to find him locked in combat with the enemy, seconds away from death. In that moment, she hadn't a thought for herself, only a deep, aching fear for the man who held her entire heart.

Charles was a solitary, secretive man who kept to himself. Over the past several days, he had been sharing more and more of his heart. If Oliver would stop interfering, their relationship could unravel naturally.

Even then, a deep-rooted fear clung to her bones. Now that she had her brother and friends with her, she worried about Charles leaving. Would he stay for her? Or would he leave her behind?

Fox tsked and leaned forward on the table, his short legs swinging beneath it. "Love knows no bounds. Even time. After hearing what you two endured together… A few weeks likely feels far longer."

True. After their time together, she felt as if she'd known Charles for months. Although he wasn't one to talk overly much, she felt like she knew his heart. Now, she wanted to know his mind.

"He's not ready."

Fox squeezed her hand. "Let him decide that."

"What?" Oliver squeaked as he shot to his feet and slammed his hands down on the table. "How did you… There's no way…"

Emmaline's mouth fell open when she spotted the smug upturn of Charles' mouth.

The man set the rest of his cards down on the table between them. Oliver swore and kicked his log chair over, hands on his hips as he turned his back to Charles and lifted his face to the sky, all while muttering profanities under his breath. He quickly spun back around and pointed a finger in Charles' face.

"Beginner's luck."

The dwarves gasped, while words still fled her tongue. Charles…won?

"Actually…" Charles leaned forward with clasped fingers resting on the table. "It's a simple strategy game. Once I learned the rules and the moves, it was only a matter of outmaneuvering you."

Oliver scowled and threw the remainder of his cards down on the table. "Best two out of three."

"You forgot to mention the stakes!" Fox called out, followed by shouts and laughter from the dwarves on all sides of her.

She kicked his foot beneath the table. This was not the time or place for this. And most of all, she couldn't bear Charles' rejection. Especially not in front of a captive audience.

Charles shrugged. "I don't have much coin on me."

"Men don't play against Ollie for money," Cub laughed, slapping his knee. "He's just so sure no one can beat him that he raises the stakes so high."

"What is it now?" Shorts asked. "Three suitors spurned for their lack of skill?"

"Three what?" Charles' eyebrows furrowed as he glanced between all of them as if trying to keep up with the conversation. Emmaline's face heated far too much to form a coherent sentence.

Oliver set his chair to rights as he grumbled, "Winning my blessing for Emmaline's hand."

Charles' tapping of a card on the table ceased suddenly. Humiliation burned her hotter. She kicked Fox again and glared at him.

"What?" Fox shrugged, speaking quietly. "I'm giving the two of you a nudge. What's the harm in that?"

"No," she hissed, leaning closer. "What you have done is doomed us. He'll never play now."

"Shuffle the cards," Charles ordered.

Emmaline inhaled sharply, her gaze snapping back to Charles. The man casually propped his elbow on the table, his chin in his hand. But he gave her a sideways glance as if gauging her reaction.

"And I can't lose my wife again!"

She recalled his words from earlier, still not having had the time to dissect his meaning. Although he'd said he hadn't meant it, he'd still spoken it. She shouldn't have hoped he could envision a future with her just like she could with him. Despite all his secrets and the burdens he kept to himself, she knew his heart. And it was good.

She focused on breathing when the next game started. What did Charles mean by this? Did he…? Could he…

Fox chuckled and nudged her with his elbow. "Doomed you, eh? I may have single-handedly saved your relationship."

But she only stared at Charles, her mouth hanging agape as they began the second game. He wasn't playing for fun anymore. He was playing for her hand.

Unfortunately, now that Oliver knew Charles could win, he was relentless in his strategy. Her heart deflated when her brother shrieked with delight and threw his cards onto the table, winning the second round.

The seriousness in Charles' eyes magnified as he frowned and gathered the cards in his hands before handing them to Skippy. "Third-party shuffle for the last round."

The area around them quieted aside from the crackling of a fire as dusk fell into evening. Skippy shuffled and dealt the cards. Tension tightened its strings around the camp. And with an anxious heart, she watched as the third round unfolded.

Both men wore serious expressions as if they faced a mirror. Whereas Oliver shifted and scratched now and again to cover up what his hand might hold, an attempt to throw

Charles off his scent, Charles remained perfectly still, not even a twitch of his face to give him away.

Emmaline knew her brother wouldn't truly give her away over a simple clash of cards. But if Charles could win, she knew it would greatly sway Oliver's respect for the man.

She held her breath as Charles laid a card between them, and the simple twitch of the corner of his mouth gave him away.

He didn't have a good hand.

Oliver drew a card next. Her brother tapped his fingers against his knee, his telltale sign that he held a good hand and he believed he was going to win.

As if feeling her gaze on him, Oliver lifted his head and met her eye across the camp.

Please, she mouthed to her brother. Oliver would ruin this for her should he win. Perhaps he might scare Charles away. And the thought of losing him broke her heart.

Oliver pressed his lips together as he glanced from his cards, to her, and back to his cards. Rather than laying his hand down, he drew another two cards.

With Charles' next turn, he laid down his hand.

And won the game.

Rather than losing his mind over defeat, Oliver offered a subdued smile and shook Charles' hand before pulling him close and whispering something in his ear, the sound drowned by her friends cheering over the win.

Charles clenched his jaw and nodded before her brother released him and busied himself with another card game with the dwarves. Fox scrambled over to the table to play. Her heart pounded dangerously hard as Charles honed in on her and approached with confident strides.

He held a hand out to her. "Walk with me?"

She could only nod as she took his strong hand and allowed him to lead her away from the others and into the darkness of the woods. Her mind spun with woozy breathlessness at his soft and tender touch, at the way his presence made her feel safe and protected.

The light of the fire slowly faded with each step away from the camp, her friends' voices growing more distant.

Heat claimed Emmaline's face, her entire body. Her heart raced at the mere contact of his hand in hers and with the anticipation of what he might say.

But so very like himself, he said nothing.

"So…" She swung their hands between them, needing something to occupy her attention other than the fiery heat that had claimed her face for the past hour and still did. "You didn't really play for my hand."

It wasn't a question. Nor a statement. But at the same time, it was almost both.

When he didn't say anything, she blushed furiously and stared at her feet as they traversed the dark path.

Continuing, she stammered, "O-O-Ollie has never found an opponent who could b-b-best him at his own game. I don't suppose he knew you enjoyed strategy games."

Still no reply.

She dropped his hand and turned back around with the intention to flee from her mortification, but before she managed to take two steps down the path, he grabbed her hand and spun her to face him dizzyingly fast. Their lips crashed together in a blazing heat of love and passion.

All the uncertainty and embarrassment melted off her shoulders as he kissed her. And when she deepened the kiss, he responded with an eager mouth.

"I'm terrible at this," he gasped against her lips. "I'm so, so sorry."

She only clutched tighter to his shirt and pulled him down for another scalding kiss. "I'd like to disagree," she replied breathlessly.

He backed her up until her shoulders brushed against a nearby tree. The heat of his body seeped into hers. His solid frame trapped her in a wall of blessed safety. His touch spurred a warmth inside her nothing could put out, and her heart responded in a fluttering mess of ecstasy.

Between kisses, he explained, "All my *relationships* have been arranged. I'm not good at this. At courting."

But he came back for more, and she accepted him without reservation. Her hands traveled up his muscular chest, over his broad shoulders, and down his arms wrapped around her waist.

"Then perhaps for once, you get to choose."

His breathy sigh tickled her lips before he bridged the gap between them once again. She kissed him without abandon. Without consequence. Her fingers threaded through his hair, pulling him closer when not even a hair's breadth lay between them in the first place.

"You are muddling my mind," he groaned before kissing the corner of her mouth, her jaw, and then her neck.

"Might I remind you that you kissed me first."

She turned her head and caught his lips in a softer kiss, one filled with sweet intent. She loved him. And she wanted to tell him. But she feared moving too quickly.

The thought nearly inspired a snort. Everything about their relationship was a quick whirlwind. But it felt beautiful and right.

Charles placed a hand on the tree trunk beside her head, breaking the kiss to stare intently into her eyes. Her stomach flipped. Her heart raced. Every fiber of her being begged to hold him close and never let go.

"This is not something I normally do," he murmured close to her but still too far. "I don't do this. I don't…"

"Kiss women in a dark forest?" she teased, poking him in the ribs.

He snorted and shook his head wryly. "I haven't kissed a woman in…a very long time. What I'm saying is I wouldn't unless it's meaningful to me. *You* mean a lot to me."

The quick beat of her heart burned with warmth at his confession. She traced his cheekbone with her fingertip and followed the outline of his jaw. "I know the presence of a beautiful woman makes you stumble over your words," she continued to jest, and he rewarded her with a smile. "But you must get more to the point. We only have so long before Ollie comes after us."

A shaky breath escaped on his exhale, and she briefly mourned his dissipating warmth as he dropped his hand and leaned away from her. "What I'm trying to say is I'm only going to kiss a woman I plan to marry."

Emmaline's lips parted, and when her world spun so suddenly, she focused on breathing slowly and allowed the tree to maintain much of her balance. "Are…are you asking for my hand?"

He blew out a long breath and shook his head. "Not yet. I want to give you the opportunity to say no."

"I won't say no," she said breathlessly before realizing just how eager and naive she sounded.

He squeezed his eyes shut and hung his head. "There are things you don't know yet. Things you deserve to hear. About me." His throat bobbed up and down. "About my family. About what I do for a living."

She trailed her fingers down his arm and gazed up at him from her position beside the tree. "It won't change my mind about you."

"You might think differently—"

"All right, you two," Oliver called from a distance, "it's been long enough!"

Emmaline silently cursed her brother's timing. She loved her brother dearly. But honestly! After so long of Charles' silence, they were finally getting somewhere, and she feared he might not open up again at another time.

She glanced back at Charles, hoping he might blurt out what was on his mind. But like she'd suspected, his expression was now guarded, his lips sealed tight.

"We'll talk again tomorrow," she promised before standing on her toes to give him one last kiss. Rather than responding with enthusiasm like earlier, she felt his hesitance. His uncertainty.

But he'd said he intended to marry her. Surely, it wasn't about a lack of feelings.

Her heart fell when she broke the kiss too soon to find a look of torturous worry on his face. *This is not about the dame. It's about the spider.* She finally understood. Something else lay hidden in his past that hurt him. And it seemed as if he feared it would hurt her, too.

"That's it!" Oliver shouted. "I'm going in there."

Tromping feet crashed through fallen leaves across the path a short distance away. Charles took her hand and pulled her back onto the path where they leisurely made their way toward him, arms lightly swinging between them.

When Oliver met them on the path, he crossed his arms, scowling when he glanced between them and then at their intertwined fingers. "I'm sure you heard me. Why didn't you answer?"

"And give our positions away should someone unfriendly hear?" Charles asked. "We were on our way back when you called."

"Uh huh," Oliver grunted, clearly not believing his words. "Gloomy has first watch, so you better get some shut eye while you can." He glanced at them again. "*Away* from each other. We'll pack up early morning and arrive home in the evening."

Unexpectedly, tears burst out of her eyes at the mention of home, and her hand flew to her mouth to try to stifle the sobs. Charles pulled her into his shoulder and comforted her with a steady hand on her back. But still, she couldn't stop the tears as she recalled the terror of getting snatched, of being threatened by knifepoint day after day, of the fear that she might truly have to endure a marriage to an old man while her family had no idea where she was. Her wall of bravery finally broke into a blubbering mess when the events of the past week caught up to her, how scared she'd been knowing she'd barely survived with Charles at her side and wouldn't have on her own.

"Ah…" Oliver said, patting her shoulder. "I didn't mean to be an arse. It wasn't my intention to make you cry."

Emmaline wiped her tears, but they kept coming. "I want to go home."

She felt rather than saw the two men share a look, and she glanced up only to catch the tail end of their silent, expressions-only conversation that men were apt to do.

Oliver squeezed her shoulder. "Do you have the strength to ride through the night? We can reach home in the morning."

When a lone tear trailed down her chin, she wiped it away. "You will all be so tired."

"It's nothing a long nap can't fix tomorrow."

"What about the horses?" But most importantly, what about Charles? Getting stabbed in the back called for rest, not travel.

Charles answered this time. "The path will be smooth enough to prevent injury, as long as we don't stray."

Despite the fatigue resting in his eyes and the pain he must be feeling in his back, he remained strong and stoic…for *her*.

She bit her lip to ward off her own tiredness. But she'd rather endure another night of little sleep than stay away from home any longer than absolutely necessary. "If you're sure…"

Without a moment's hesitation, the two led her back to camp, and Oliver shouted to the others, "Pack up, boys! The princess demands an immediate carriage back home."

"Ollie!" she giggled with a roll of her eyes, and she glanced to the side to find Charles fighting his own smile as he played along by holding out a hand to help her onto the horse. Her other friends met the enthusiasm with a "hoorah!"

She was the farthest thing from a princess, but for a few hours, she didn't mind pretending.

Chapter Twelve

The sky lightened enough to give Emmaline a view of the path ahead. The same dirt path. Dark silhouettes of trees. But the scent of smoke, leather, and sweet food knocked the air from her lungs with a punch of nostalgia.

Her eyes smarted when their group broke through the trees and entered a giant clearing filled with rows of colorful tents topped with triangle flags fluttering in a light breeze. A dozen of her family members were already going about their day in the early morning. Some practiced their juggling. Others trained with the animals. And when one of them spotted her…

Chaos ensued.

Her family rushed at her, pulling her from the horse and into a sea of warm, familiar embraces. Questions hit her right and left, ones she found herself unable to answer when her throat constricted with emotion.

Charles had done this. He'd kept his promise and escorted her home. She owed him her life. She owed him everything.

But then everyone quieted, and thick tension filled the air.

"Why have you brought him here?" Madame Gina thundered, storming out of one of the tents in a flurry of skirts, hooped earrings, and a stern expression, her gaze jumping between her and Charles.

"I don't understand." She grabbed his arm and held him firmly in her grip. "Charles saved my life. I would have been long dead without him."

A round of murmurs lifted into the air around them, but when she glanced at Charles, his lips were pressed together, his expression hard as he turned his head away from her. Was he embarrassed?

No, shame looked more like what rested in his eyes. But why?

"Charles is not a Charles at all," Madame Gina said, nostrils flaring. "I never forget a face. And I know I have seen his before. Years ago. But it was younger then." She lifted a hand and gestured to the man. "He's the crowned prince of Armandy. Prince Christopher Avington."

Shocked silence.

Charles tried to lift his gaze, but it felt heavy, laden with so much burden piled up over the course of his lifetime. He'd tried so hard to escape his past. Why did it have to follow him here? Why did she have to remember his face?

"Tell me it's not true," Emmaline murmured, clutching onto his arm as if desperate to believe the lie.

Without looking at her, he answered in a husky, heavy tone. "I told you I didn't want you to hate me. Especially after learning what happened to your family. You told me you could never. But you didn't truly understand."

Slowly, her hand dropped to her side, and only then did he find the strength to lift his head to find her expression filled with shock. With betrayal. But how could he have told her the truth? He wanted to bury Christopher Avington. Forever.

He spoke to the group as a whole, revealing the entire truth with heaviness and exhaustion rather than anger.

"I married a lovely woman named Lillian. I was young. Too young. And naive. The marriage was arranged, but I was happy. She was the daughter of one of my father's friends. The man was a baron." He ran a hand over his chin as he forced himself to relive the tale. Just one more time. "My father and his friend had a falling out, which soured the marriage in my father's eyes. Another offer came along. For an alliance between Armandy and a neighboring kingdom. But…I was twenty and married. My younger brothers were too young for marriage."

A shuddering breath escaped him. He felt pressure building in his chest. A stinging sensation behind his eyes.

Madame Gina nodded for him to continue.

"Lillian was due any day, and my father felt threatened by the child. Should it be born a boy, it would become the next heir in my reign. So." His words trembled. He was not going to make it through the tale. He hadn't cried in many years, but he was going to ugly weep. He could feel it.

Warm fingers slipped through his, and he glanced down at Emmaline and the concerned pinch of her mouth. Because she knew what came next. Her comfort gave him enough strength to continue.

"My father wanted this new alliance over what we currently had, to create a stronger tie. He tried to do it in secret, to make it look like an accident, but I figured it out. I—" His voice cracked, and he took a moment to steady his emotions. "He ordered my brother to take me on a fool's errand, leaving Lillian without protection. And with me gone and distracted, my father killed her."

He clenched his fist, recalling finding her bloodied body on the floor—

His mind blocked out the rest. "I abdicated the throne after we buried her and my son. And I assure you, I have made him pay for what he's done to me." He only wished he could have made him pay more. "My family is dead to me. I will not go by a name they chose for me. I am Charles Lockwood. Christopher Avington is dead."

Immediately, Madame Gina's expression changed into one of sympathy. "Oh, you poor boy. Just like many of us here. Your past is filled with blood and loss." She pulled him into a motherly embrace. "That man has wronged so many."

His chest tightened. His eyes stung. He was going to burst into tears at any moment. And he didn't want an audience when it happened.

"I'm tired," he murmured, stepping away from the woman. "Am I welcome to stay here? Or would you like me to leave?"

"Stay," Emmaline and Madame Gina said at the same time.

The older woman started shooing them away. "Show him to the supply tent for now. It's quiet there. We'll make other sleeping arrangements tonight."

Charles was losing the fight to keep his emotions hidden and locked up tight. Silent tears trailed down his face as Emmaline led him by the hand toward a lone, white and red tent standing erect next to several larger ones. He turned his head toward the trees in an attempt to keep her from seeing the heartache spilling from his eyes. But judging by the way she said nothing and kept stealing glances at him, she noticed.

She gently guided him by the hand into the tent where ropes, hoops, canvas, and more lay in a semi-organized manner throughout the small space. She urged him to sit on a stone bench and excused herself to fetch him water.

His body slumped. His shoulders shook. He hid his face in his hands to try to stifle the sobs leaking through his lips. Memories flashed through his mind the way they did when he spoke of what happened. Violent, harrowing memories that ceaselessly attacked his mind as if he lived through the event again and again. The blood. The heartache and agony. The pain of loss. And the burning desire for revenge.

The memories consumed him, of the day he'd died and came back as something…else. The event had changed him forever. Gone was the innocent, naive young man whose world was bright and filled with so much possibility. The pure goodness had died with Lillian. His blind trust. His optimistic attitude. His desire to see the good in others. It was all gone. Turned to ash.

And the world felt so much…darker.

A hand on his shoulder startled him out of the past and into the present. He inhaled sharply and glanced up to find a blurred version of a woman with blonde, curly hair and a kind, gentle face. Her hand smoothed across his cheek to his chin before she sat down beside him and guided his head onto her lap.

The kind gesture caused a choked sob to escape him, and soon enough, he couldn't stop himself from weeping out every pent-up emotion he'd shouldered for six years.

"I didn't want to tell you like this," he choked, wishing he hadn't been forced to reveal the darkness of his past to people he didn't know. "This was supposed to be private."

"I'm sorry it happened this way," she murmured as her fingers stroked his hair.

"You must hate me."

Her silence nearly confirmed his fears, but then her words calmed the anxiety in his heart. "I'm shocked. And I feel a little…stupid. Here I thought you were a mercenary or an assassin. I never thought I was traveling with a prince."

"I'm not a prince anymore." He hiccupped and choked on another sob, feeling ridiculous for breaking down now of all times. He hadn't cried in years. And now he couldn't stop the tears. "I should be allowed to bury my past identity without needing to tell everyone the truth."

She shifted beneath him, only to kiss him on the temple. More tears escaped as hot trails over the bridge of his nose.

"My family will keep your secret. I promise you that." Another kiss. "We all have secrets, and we're closer because of it."

He lifted his hand to rest on her knee, still keeping his head faced away from her. "You terrify me," he whispered when his weeping died down to quiet sniffles and silent tears.

Her hand stilled on his hair. "Why?"

"Because I want that with you. Family." He swallowed as he forced the truth from his mouth. "And that scares me."

Her touch moved to trace his ear. "I still don't know what that looks like. You are still keeping a lot from me."

So many secrets. So many things he'd buried. So many things he'd become.

However, the worst part was hearing the hesitancy in her voice. She'd told him she wouldn't say no. But she hadn't known the entire truth then. What would she say after he told her everything? Laid his heart bare? Allowed himself to become vulnerable and give his fragile trust to her? Would she break it? Or keep it safe?

He sat up, scrubbing his face with his hands as he tried to figure out where to start. Fatigue rested in his eyes, on his shoulders, weighing down his entire body. But he couldn't allow another moment to pass before he told her what she needed to know.

"How did you make your father pay?" she prompted when he remained silent for a beat too long.

He hunched his shoulders when keeping his wounded back upright pained him. "I rode off into the night, on the trail for weeks, running from the people he sent after me. And then I rode into enemy territory." He chuckled humorlessly and gave her a pointed look. "If you are wanting to keep all your secrets, you shouldn't anger your heir." He shook his head and sighed. "The Edilann king nearly killed me for venturing onto his land, but he gave me a chance. I spilled all my father's secrets. How many were in his army. Who his spies were. Battle tactics. Crafted treaties. Plans for future attack. I left my father *nothing*. I only regret not seeing his face when he realized *who* spilled his secrets."

"I wish I could say I condemn your behavior, but I can't."

He chuckled darkly. "As the heir, my father taught me everything he knew. I never intended turning on him and my kingdom until he turned on me."

She rubbed his shoulder soothingly. "That still doesn't explain why you decided to rescue a not-princess from a certain death. Why were you there that day?"

He supposed it required a lot more explaining. He knew he should say nothing. But…it was Emmaline. He trusted her. He needed her to know.

"After I spilled the secrets, the king locked me up for a time, which was surprising considering I expected him to kill me. I had no thought for myself through this ordeal. I just wanted revenge."

And he still didn't regret it. The revenge. It felt like justice to him. Freedom.

Continuing, he said, "When the Edilann king realized everything I told him was true…" He laughed breathlessly, feeling more free than he'd felt in a long time. The weight sitting on his chest was gone. "He asked me to work for him." Now, Charles spoke slowly, waiting for her reaction. "To keep from using my real name, they call me Huntsman."

Her lips parted as she glanced back and forth between his eyes. "So…you *are* an assassin."

He shook his head. "No, but King Royce certainly is trying to get me to do some dirty deeds."

Such as kill her. But he certainly wasn't going to follow through.

"Then…then what are you?"

He lowered his voice. "I am a spy for the king of Edilann. For King Royce Winfield."

"A spy?" she gasped. "What were you doing guarding Princess Isobel?"

He shrugged again at the obvious. "Gathering information about the royal family. I got more than I bargained for." His mouth twitched on one side, and in turn, she laughed and playfully shoved his shoulder.

Oh, he should have spilled his heart ages ago. He felt so light. So free. So…happy.

"I am forbidden to tell anyone of my true profession other than my fiancée or wife. Even then, it's discouraged."

Emmaline stared at him for a long moment. "Then why are you telling me?"

His mouth twitched as he turned his head to the side. "I suppose I'm holding onto the hope that you won't say no." He chuckled and shook his head when she only gaped at him. "I know I've given you a lot to think about." He reached out to her and cupped her hands between his. "I've shunned women and relationships. I shouldn't want a life with you. But I do. And I'll answer any questions you have. I'll be completely transparent."

"You knew the woman who attacked you. Who was she?"

"We used to work together. Her name is Poisoner. She's a double-crosser spy who works for Leonia."

She nodded slowly as if taking in the information. "Has the king of Armandy tried to come after you?"

A part of him appreciated her using the man's title rather than calling him his father. "Multiple times. But I'm under the Edilann king's protection. He gave up years ago. He's no threat to me anymore."

"You are sure?"

He understood her hesitancy. A life of running, of looking over one's shoulder, was no life at all. "I am. Short of waging war over an abdicated heir… There is nothing he can do."

"And…your friends you mentioned. Do they know who you are?"

He scoffed at the thought of Barnaby, Tobie, and Edward. "No, they don't know. Can you imagine how they'd react after learning I'm the king's spy?" He scratched his chin, fighting against the fatigue growing heavier on his shoulders. "They'd distrust me. Besides, I don't rat them out and never will. I first made friends with them to protect my identity. But… They became important to me. They accept me as I am and don't ask questions. They're all I have. I have no one else."

Emmaline brushed her fingers over his and drew circles on the back of his hand. "You have me."

He turned his head and held her gaze, trying to pick apart the things she didn't say. There were a lot of things she didn't speak of, a lot of questions she didn't ask. He felt…uncertain. Unsure of himself. He hated this feeling, not truly knowing where he stood with her.

"Please keep what I told you between us. Not even Oliver should know."

A troubled look crossed her eyes, but still, she nodded. "What do you tell everyone your occupation is?"

"Trade. Keeps me wealthy enough to walk among nobles without a title, and no one questions my frequent involvement with the king."

To his disappointment, she dropped his hand and stood from the bench. "Answer me one last question."

He gestured for her to continue.

"Do you love your job?"

She faced away from him, preventing him from seeing her expression. The question seemed… misplaced… considering the current conversation.

Turning away from her, he stared down at his hands resting between his knees. "Emma, I had nothing else. I came to Edilann as a fugitive, as a refugee, as the enemy. I started out with nothing. I've given up so much for this life. I've *lost* so much for this life." He swallowed and lifted his gaze, only to find her attention fixed on him. "Yes, I love this job. Because it has given me a new life with choices and freedom I didn't have otherwise."

She stepped closer to him, taking him by surprise as she lifted his chin and placed a kiss directly beneath his eye where his freckle resided. Next, she lightly kissed his lips, and just the simple caress was enough to calm the anxiety, the uncertainty in his spirit.

He should have pulled her closer, to deepen their contact and kiss her senseless. But he was exhausted, and his back ached like nothing he'd experienced in a long time. Therefore, he settled for pressing her palm to his cheek and squeezing her fingers.

"You've given me a lot to think about," she murmured when they broke apart. "I know you're tired. Get some rest. I'll hopefully see you tonight."

"What's tonight?"

A smile lingered on her face as she approached the exit of the tent, pausing at the flap to glance back at him. "There's a performance after dusk. And I'll most definitely be on stage."

Chapter Thirteen

mmaline shoved the red and white flaps open to the main tent, storming inside where her family was setting up for the performance later that night. They stopped what they were doing, watching her as she paced.

"He's a prince!" She threw her hands up as the shock of the revelation finally caught up to her. "A storming, royal, blazing prince! What do I do? I don't know what to do!"

Her friend, Susan, took her by the shoulders and squeezed, a strand of dark brown hair falling over the large, purple birthmark on half her face. She blew it away from her eyes with a gust of breath. "What does every prince need?"

"A princess," she gasped, feeling light-headed. "I'm not a princess. I'm just a misfit nutter nobody who will never be a somebody!"

"Whoa," Skippy said with a shake of his head. A silly hat rested on top of his head while he unicycled circles around them with two of his dwarf companions. "You don't give yourself enough credit."

Julian, a man so tall that she had to crane her neck upward, cracked a whip through the air with a practiced movement. "You're more of a princess than anyone I've ever met."

She might have laughed through her hysterics if the panic hadn't won over first. "I can't do this. I can't do it."

"Take a deep breath," Susan ordered, and she attempted to follow her lead as they breathed in deeply and let it out. "You're our best singer. We'll just have to show him that he can't live without you."

Oliver burst out of the racks of clothing with a big smile on his face as he carried a pile of blue cloth. "I think I heard someone say princess. Or was I mistaken?"

Everyone let out a collective "oooh" at the way the dress shimmered and sparkled like stars in the night sky. Her brother handed her a pair of soft, elbow-length gloves the color of midnight jewels.

Her eyes smarted at the beautiful gown once belonging to a queen from a faraway kingdom. Madame Gina had found it washed up on the shore, soggy within a wooden chest. Or so the story went. It was too special to wear.

"I can't," she insisted, shaking her head. "Not for him. I know many of you probably think it's hard having him here."

Madame Gina approached with a crystal-jeweled crown and tucked it into the strands of her hair. "He was just a boy when the king attacked my people. And he was only a young man when the king attacked yours. *Charles* is innocent, a victim just like the rest of us. I wish I could say the same for his family." The woman straightened the crown and stepped back with a smile. "If he makes you happy, then I hope the stars align tonight to give you the happy beginning you deserve."

Beginning. Not ending. Madame Gina liked to call every new adventure a new beginning. A fresh start. Another chance at happiness.

"I'm not a princess," she whispered.

"And he's not technically a prince," Oliver replied with a giant grin on his face. He held up the dress. "But tonight, you will dazzle Sir Charming."

She laughed at the title, especially because Charles *wasn't* that charming at all, but rather quiet and gruff and calculating and perhaps a bit cold. But he was sweet and kind. Protective and strong. He made her feel things she hadn't known she could feel. The warmth he brought to her life…the happiness.

She loved him, and she knew there was no one else she wanted at her side.

When she held out her arms, her family rushed in and held her in a tight group embrace. They meant everything to her. She was so lucky to have them in her life.

Charles groaned.

His back ached something fierce. His eyes burned from not getting enough sleep. His body begged him to roll back over and allow himself to return to a fitful slumber.

But whistling music, pounding drums, and loud laughter outside the storage tent gave him pause.

He bolted upright and hissed when the sharp pain in his back nearly grounded him. For several long moments, he focused on taking deep breaths, pushing through the throbbing pain between his shoulders. Although it hurt, he counted himself lucky the blade hadn't been poisoned. One of Poisoner's men must have managed to stab him instead of the woman herself.

A frown pulled on his mouth as he ran a hand over his scraggly face. Several weeks had passed since he'd shaved. His clothing was dirty, grimy, and a bit stiff from going so long without bathing. Not to mention the layers of mud caked to his boots.

He was a sore sight.

And now, especially, he didn't want to look like a homeless potato when the probability of running into Emmaline soon was rather high.

Bracing himself against the ground, he started to stand when he caught sight of the corner of a paper sticking out from the tarp he'd rested his head on. His eyebrows drew together as he unfolded the paper to find words staring back at him, written in an unsure, shaky hand. Many letters were backward. Others misspelled. But he managed to make out what it said.

Charles,

For all you told me this morning, you sure do sleep like a log. You really are full of surprises, but I do enjoy when someone keeps me on my toes.

I'm performing tonight, and before you get upset with me, just know that I will not push myself beyond my limits. I hope you will be able to make it. If you wake up in time. There may be something sweet in it for you if you find me after the performance.

All my heart,
Emma

He laughed, his smile lingering as he traced the closing of the letter with his thumb. He felt it sure in his bones. She felt the same way he did. And he knew without a doubt they belonged together. Being with her felt right. She chased his darkness away and filled his soul with happiness. Although he didn't know what a future with her looked like, he knew he wanted to try.

A pit of nervousness crawled through his stomach as he sifted through the storage tent until he found shaving supplies and clean cloth. He wanted to stay here in Leonia with her troupe. At least for a time. But his most recent assignment took precedence. No more time remained for him to leisurely travel about the countryside with Emmaline. He needed to return home. At least until he reported to the king and took on his next assignment.

Only one question remained… Would Emmaline come with him? Or would she stay? Because he didn't know when he'd be able to come back.

Either tonight they would seal the deal, or they might have to discover what a long-distance relationship looked like for them.

His heart raced, his stomach flipping and flopping as he shaved, cleaned himself with the water and cloth, and located clean clothing tucked away that he suspected might be a costume. But it looked just like what he usually wore in

Edilann, so he slipped on the black trousers, white tunic, and buttoned up the embroidered navy-blue vest, finishing with wiping his boots clean until not a speck of dirt remained.

The last time he'd felt so nervous was his wedding day. Since losing Lillian, nothing had scared him. Not combat or sneaking into a place he wasn't supposed to be. But Emmaline made him nervous. He felt terrified. But he took comfort in knowing he'd already made his intentions clear. She knew he would propose, and that he would do it soon.

If only he had enough faith that she'd say yes.

He fixed his unruly hair last before standing near the exit while muffled laughter and voices lay on the other side of the flaps. He took a deep breath.

And stepped outside.

His own sharp intake of breath stopped him in his tracks when the large clearing was unrecognizable compared to what he'd witnessed only hours ago. Hundreds of people ambled about, talking excitedly amongst themselves. The loose-fitting sleeves of many of them indicated most hailed from Leonia. But there were a select few wearing vests or corsets like those of Edilann. When the troupe lay close to the other kingdom's borders, he wasn't surprised to find them here.

He craned his neck to look over the crowd. He spotted an enormously tall man from the troupe twirling fire on a baton with a captive audience. Several of the dwarves performed their own neat trick of juggling while riding unicycles. But most of the people made their way toward the largest tent, slowly trickling inside into the unknown.

Charles searched the vicinity for a head of blonde hair. Finding none resembling the person he wanted to see, he followed the crowd into the large tent, and the darkness quickly swallowed him. Numerous bodies pressed against him on all sides as people tried to shove their way closer to the front.

He frowned, disliking the contact. His gaze darted about the sea of people until he spotted a wooden support beam helping to hold up the tent. He slipped in and out of small gaps until he reached the beam, grabbed onto the rough wood, and hauled himself up until one leg rested on the beam and the other dangled over the side.

At the front of the tent lay red drapes with golden tassels. Beneath the tassels, movement of several pairs of feet caught his eye as if he sat at the theater, waiting for the next act to come onto the stage.

Horns blew to announce the beginning of the performance. All at once, the audience quieted with anticipation. And when a variety of instruments played in earnest somewhere behind the stage, a group of four ladies shuffled out. His jaw dropped at their scanty outfits covered in crystals and feathers, but most especially at their net-clad legs and high-heeled shoes, leaving hardly anything to the imagination.

The ladies fluttered fans made of feathers as they began dancing in a synchronized line along to the music. His stomach twisted when he spotted curly blonde hair beneath a black-net hat covering half the woman's face.

Emmaline.

He would recognize her anywhere. The way she moved. The smile on her lips. The elegant turns of her wrists. He found himself torn between wanting to cover her up and watching in awe at the way she moved fluidly, in sync with the other dancers.

She held his attention captive as he watched the way she kicked and spun and fluttered her feathered fan. Her gaze jumped about as if in search of someone. A part of him hoped she wanted to find him in the crowd. But he doubted she would look in the rafters.

He blinked.

And she was gone.

He scanned the stage below but found no hint of her presence as other performers entered with animals and other acrobatic acts. Two performers held a cloth between them while another stood on top of it, getting thrown into the air and performing all sorts of incredible feats like twirls and flips, his feet finding the cloth again on his way down.

The audience cheered wildly.

Act after act passed, leaving him both amazed and reeling from disbelief. How could they perform such daring feats and not get injured?

And then another hush fell upon the audience as one of the performers carried a small set of stairs out onto the stage. The light around the audience dimmed, and the torches around the stage billowed a brilliant blue.

Several long moments passed when nothing happened, but the tension in the air only increased tenfold.

Music started once again behind the stage, slower this time, with what he guessed was a flute and perhaps a fiddle.

The red drapes pulled back to expose a woman dressed in a sparkling dark blue gown with a long train trailing behind her with each slow step. His breath caught when he barely recognized Emmaline as she lifted an elbow-length gloved hand to brush a strand of blonde curls out of her eyes, the perfectly coiffed strands adorned with a sparkling crystal crown.

She opened her mouth to sing, and he nearly lost his balance on the rafters when the beautiful sound struck him straight through the heart. His eyes widened in absolute awe at the way the dress sparkled as she climbed the set of stairs until she stood at the top, her voice easily carrying throughout the tent.

Emotion clogged his throat as his gaze trailed over the lovely woman on the stage, as his ears took in her beautiful voice. He loved everything about her. Her wild and confident spirit. Her drive. Her kind, sweet heart.

Love…

His heart whispered the word, as if uttering anything louder might have him fleeing with his tail tucked between his legs. Little by little, he'd fallen in love with her, but he'd only been absolutely sure when she'd stood over him with a dagger in hand, protecting him from Poisoner. She'd risked her own life to save him.

And he loved her for it.

He couldn't help but chuckle, a wide grin spreading across his face when he realized he wasn't the only man falling in love with her tonight, judging by the awe in plenty more eyes than just his own.

Emmaline finished the song with a drawn-out note, simultaneously making his heart ache and soar.

The crowd roared with applause. He whistled and clapped, quickly climbing down from the rafters to make his way toward her. But as his gaze landed on the stage, she was gone.

When the crowd pushed and shoved their way out of the tent, he had no choice but to follow the stampede until he stumbled outside into the fresh air. The buzz of excitement swirled around him, but he tuned out the noise as he searched for Emmaline.

He caught sight of Fox on his unicycle, and the moment their gazes met, the other man motioned with his head toward another tent around the back.

Nervous excitement caught in his chest, and he tried his hardest not to sprint to her supposed location. Or away from it. His legs felt like jelly, bound to collapse at any moment with terrifying anticipation.

His eyebrows shot up in surprise when he found another tent behind the large one. Flowers littered every speck of free space in front of the tent while shouting males vied for Emmaline's attention.

Oliver and several of the dwarves stood at the front of the tent, arms crossed, guarding the structure as if this wasn't the first time they'd had to do it.

Hesitantly, Charles approached, unsure whether he'd be turned away like the others or allowed through.

When Oliver caught sight of him, his mouth twitched into a smirk as he motioned with his head toward the tent flaps. "I've been denying all her other admirers entrance to see her. But I suppose I can make an exception for you."

Charles grimaced when his gaze landed on the dozens of bouquets of flowers, realizing he had nothing to offer her. Nothing at all. No flowers. No ring. Nothing but his love and a promise. "I finally understand why you make her admirers play for her hand. I didn't realize she had so many."

The other man shrugged, his smirk only growing wider. "What did you expect? Beautiful, talented women are fawned over, and Emma is one of a kind."

When Charles started forward, Oliver grasped his arm and leaned closer, a dangerous, protective look in his eyes. "Only you," he warned. "Do not betray my trust."

"I won't, I swear."

After a moment, Oliver nodded and released his arm.

Taking a deep breath, he lifted one of the flaps and ducked inside the tent.

Emmaline paced back and forth, back and forth, while wringing one of her gloves between her hands. She hadn't seen Charles at the performance. All her efforts to capture his attention could have been for naught, as he might have slept through the entire thing, anyway.

"Emma," a deep voice said behind her, "you were magnificent."

She gasped and spun around, her heart in her throat when she faced a stranger. But then her heart calmed when she realized he wasn't a stranger at all. He just looked *different.*

Her gaze swept over Charles' nice clothing to his clean-shaven face and his well-kept hair. He was far more handsome than she'd ever seen him. And it intimidated her. Because he no longer looked like a rugged soldier on the trail. He looked like…he looked like…

A *prince.*

"Charles!" she breathed, a hand flying to her heart as she looked him up and down. Warmth bloomed in her cheeks when she met his gaze once again. "I didn't recognize you. You startled me."

"Because I'm not covered in dirt and sweat?" he jested in a dry tone.

"Well…yes. No beard. Your hair looks nice. And you look…" The heat in her face spread to the rest of her body. "Regal."

And suddenly, she felt small standing next to him. Small and intimidated. A bit shy. Unfit to do anything more than fall into a curtsy and submit to his authority. It didn't matter that she wore a gown befitting a princess. She felt like an imposter in his presence. Because he radiated confidence, authority, and wealth.

And her?

She was nothing.

Her gaze lowered to the ground when she found herself on unsteady, unequal footing. Charles was a prince by birthright. He'd grown up as a royal, as the king's *heir*. She must seem so…so little in comparison. A joke. Because someone like him could have any woman he wanted, surely. Why would he want *her*?

"I'm usually a bit scruffy," he said, breaking her out of her despondent daze with the sound of his voice. "Just feels nice to be clean. It's been several weeks of bathing from the rain alone."

Another jest. But she couldn't bring herself to smile. Not when her heart pounded a sad, pitiful rhythm as her mind tortured her with the reminder of everything she lacked.

Charles stepped closer and gently trapped her chin in his fingers, lifting her head. The half-smile he offered her was dazzling. Like a chandelier glimmering like jewels within a grand ballroom.

"The way this usually goes is with a third-party negotiator." He chuckled and shook his head, and his fingers moved from her chin to brush her cheek. "I'm going to muddle this, and I've already accepted I'm going to muddle it."

"Charles," she tried to protest, but his name escaped more like a breathy pleading.

"I've laid my heart bare. I've told you things I've never told anyone. I've stripped myself down to nothing. Because I...I..." He swallowed and quirked his mouth side to side. "I care about you so much. You are radiant and breathtaking and have the voice of an angel. Marry me, Emma."

Marry me...

Her lungs deflated with a whoosh of breath. Her eyes pricked with emotion until his face blurred before her. She answered with the only words she knew she could.

"I can't."

Charles stared at Emmaline with a slack jaw, blinking several times as he tried to make sense of her answer. It wasn't what he had expected to escape her lips, especially after all the sweet words they'd exchanged. The kisses they'd shared.

"I need time," she murmured hurriedly. "You must understand."

His heart cracked as his hands slowly released her and dropped to his sides. He adopted the emotionless mask he'd perfected over the years, betraying nothing of his feelings nor his thoughts.

For six years, he'd shunned relationships, vowing never to court and especially never to marry. He'd broken his vow, only to burn himself in the end. When he'd been a prince, the courtships of his friends and himself had always been short before an engagement or marriage. At least within his circle. Despite knowing his courtship with Emmaline had been short, this was how it was done to his knowledge.

He also had no more time to give before he was to return home.

"Right." He cleared his throat and stepped back. "I understand." He would not try again. This was it for them. The end of the line. The brittle wall of love and trust he'd built crumbled at his feet, and he watched it happen with a dead expression. His heart was too fragile to have attempted to build a life with her, to woo her and court her. It was better to not have a heart at all than to give it to someone who didn't want it.

"Charles." She frowned and made a grab for him, but he jerked out of reach. "This is not a no. I just need time."

"And I said I understand."

Nothing more needed to be said. She'd given her answer. And he was a fool with a broken heart.

"This is my family, Charles." Her expression fell as she crossed her arms over herself. "I can't leave them."

"I never asked you to."

Family… The word slashed his chest like a whip over his heart. He wanted to be that for her. But she just made it clear that he wasn't. And he could never be.

Laughter broke out on the opposite wall of the tent, causing her to jump. She turned as her gaze leaped toward the sound, and he took that moment to slip out of the tent before she managed to turn back to him.

He melded into the crowd with practiced ease, ignoring Oliver when he called after him. Because when he didn't want to be found…

He wouldn't be.

Chapter Fourteen

Sob after sob broke through Emmaline's resolve to stay strong. But her will crumpled when she found a single letter on her pillow. The sight shot dread straight to her toes. Although she didn't recognize the elegant handwriting, she immediately knew it was from Charles.

Emmaline –

It has been a long time since I've been home. I'm afraid I can't afford to stay away any longer. I have a job to finish and loose ends to tie up. You were beautiful up on that stage. It's where you belong. I can see that now. With your family and all your adoring fans.

Please stay safe. Keep someone with you at all times for a few weeks at least, or until your troupe crosses the border.

It was a pleasure to know you, Emma. I will make sure to see your next show should you end up in Edilann.

Take care.
Charles

A second, smaller piece of parchment fell out of the letter and onto her lap.

In case Oliver wanted to finish that game fair and square. Game-throwers are hardly better than game-cheaters.

Below the words was an address located in Edilann.

Emmaline's hand flew to her mouth, her heart shattering into her lap. Charles was gone. And rather than saying goodbye in person, he'd given her a letter. It was more than she deserved.

Without bothering to announce himself, her brother threw open the flaps leading to her section of the women's tent, a frown puckering his mouth. "Where did Charles go? He rode off on his horse. He wouldn't answer my questions."

Tears still dripping down her face, she silently handed her brother the letter from Charles.

Oliver scoffed after a few moments. "I can't believe he knew I threw the game."

"Ollie!" she wept. "That's beside the point."

He tossed the letter onto her pillow. "So, what happened? I tried to eavesdrop, but your admirers were too loud."

She yanked the crown out of her hair and threw off her gloves, which landed beside her on the cot. "It all happened so suddenly. He asked for my hand. If I had more time to prepare…" She sniffed and swiped at her cheeks.

"You had all night to prepare!"

"He intimated me!"

Her brother's gaze darkened. "How?"

Embarrassment caught onto tongue, causing her to stutter. "H-h-he looked so h-h-handsome. Like a p-p-prince."

"Yeah, yeah, yeah. We were all aware of how handsome he was." He rolled his eyes. "That was the whole idea of turning you into a princess tonight!" he exclaimed, throwing his hands up in the air. "To get him to propose. Why did you throw this away?"

"I didn't turn him down," she wept, wiping tear after tear away. "I only said I needed more time."

"And he took it as a rejection," her brother stated.

She nodded. "I know his heart is fragile. I should have handled this better. But there is so much to consider. I love my life here. He has a good occupation. And his past makes things difficult. I need to understand better what I would be subjecting myself to. And…and…how can we make things work between us?" She whispered her greatest insecurity. "He's a prince. I don't belong with someone like that. Look at me!"

"*Was* a prince."

"It doesn't matter! He was married to the love of his life. How can I compete with that when I'm *me*? Misfit little me who sings and dances and performs and doesn't belong in his world."

"Charles said the marriage was arranged. He never said the woman was his heart and soul. Besides, you don't even know what his world looks like," he argued. "You haven't given him a chance to show you."

She threw her hands up. "Oh, now you are on his side?"

"I am on *your* side!" He pointed a finger into her face. His blue eyes sparked with annoyance. "You are sabotaging yourself. You clearly love the man."

"That was *before* I found out who he really is—was." She covered her face with a shaky hand before slumping back onto her cot. "I'm scared, Ollie. I'm not the kind of woman who is right for him."

"And how do you know that? Don't you think he knows better what is right for him than you do?"

Shaking her head, she glared at him. "That's not a fair accusation."

He rolled his eyes and gestured to the tent's exit. "Charles is clearly ready to move on after what happened back when. How long do you think he will remain on the marriage market?" He shrugged his shoulders. "A man like that is not a man who will be available for long. He's every woman's fancy."

"And yours, too, it seems," she teased, wiping her eyes.

"Ha-ha." He kicked her foot. And then once more as if to make his point.

She buried her face in her hands when she found herself unable to put the pieces of her heart back together. She recalled Charles' rare smiles and laughter, the intense way he protected her, his 'nothing was impossible' view on life. She loved every look he gave her. Every touch. His quiet, calm presence. The way he filled her life with joy and sunshine.

Now, it was as if a large, thick raincloud blocked the sunlight. She needed him in her life. Her brother was right. Why had she thrown this away?

"What am I going to do?" she whispered, wiping her eyes again. "I think I made a mistake."

Oliver placed a hand on her shoulder. "The question you should really ask is… What are *we* going to do?"

I'm an idiot, Charles thought to himself, caught between self-deprecation and absolute embarrassment. He'd born his heart and soul to Emmaline. All for what? While she stood there and smiled, waiting for the perfect opportunity to let him down gently.

He'd thought they were on the same page. She'd told him she wouldn't say no. She'd led him to believe she might feel the same for him as he did for her.

Was she trying to make a fool out of me? a quieter voice asked deeper in his mind. The part where fear and uncertainty ran rampant, without restraint. Now that he thought back on it, the only thing she'd said to him was she appreciated him. His poor, lonely soul had tried to make it into something when it clearly meant something else to her entirely.

"This is why I swore off women," he grumbled, tightening his grip on the horse's reins as they tromped through the dim atmosphere on their way back to Edilann. But when the creature nickered in protest, he relaxed his muscles. "So they couldn't hurt me."

Yet, the ache in his chest hurt far worse than the ache between his shoulder blades. In the space of weeks, he'd gone from detesting Emmaline to protecting her to loving her. And now he was the one paying for his foolish heart.

A long sigh heaved from his lungs when it began raining. Again. He picked up the horse's pace to try to gain as much ground as possible before the roads became muddy. The way ahead was visible in the early morning light, also traversed by many others trying to seek shelter from the oncoming storm.

He sighed again and reined his mount down another path when the way toward the city was clogged with too many people whose carts were getting stuck in the mud. After a few minutes, he rode through a tunnel of trees before spotting an enormous estate up ahead belonging to his friend, Barnaby Mavis.

Shivering from the cold, he handed his horse to a stable hand who had seen him coming before jogging up the steps to the estate. The head butler opened the door for him, and when he slipped inside the warm structure, he released another sigh, but this one of relief.

Servants quietly bustled around the estate, as quiet as shadows and just as fleeting. One of them led him to a room while another servant finished lighting a fire in the hearth.

He chuckled under his breath, forgetting what being wealthy and titled felt like. He'd definitely stepped down a peg or two, but he didn't mind.

Only a few minutes passed before a servant brought him a plate of fruits, breads, cheeses, and jams. He settled down on a soft, red-velvet chair and kicked his feet up in front of the hearth. This wasn't even his home, but they still treated a friend like royalty.

On the opposite side of the room, his friend, Barnaby, walked in with messy blond hair while wearing a red robe over his sleep clothes. His wife, Ivette, blinked sleepily, her copper strands a stark contrast to the white robe she wore over her white nightgown.

Barnaby grinned from ear to ear and held out his arms. "Charles! I haven't seen you in months!"

The two briefly embraced, and Ivette gave him a longer embrace and a platonic kiss on the cheek.

"What are you doing here?" the man asked, nodding toward his rumpled, slightly damp clothing. "Your house is only twenty minutes away."

"I couldn't make it."

He was sick and tired of traveling in wet clothing and wanted to avoid it again if possible. Besides, if he made it home, his journey would officially end. He didn't want to let go of Emmaline yet.

"What took you so long?" Barnaby asked as they pulled up chairs beside the hearth while the servants ducked out of the room. "I thought you said you'd return weeks ago."

Perhaps so, but…

"I met a woman," he said slowly, carefully, his gaze darting toward the flames to avoid looking them in the eye. "She turned me down."

Ivette's expression was compassionate as she patted his hand. "I'm sorry to hear it."

Unlike his wife, Barnaby made a face, blatant disbelief in his eyes. "Umm…*why?*"

Charles shrugged and picked at one of the loose buttons on his vest he still needed to return to the troupe. "I don't think she likes…who I am." He didn't give any more information, hoping the others wouldn't press for details.

But then Barnaby surprised him by laughing, sharing a look with his wife. "You think we don't know who you are?" He grinned and stole a piece of bread off Charles' tray and spread jam across the slice. "Of course, whatever you do on the side is a mystery, and I think you're a bit strange…"

"You never did tell us why you stole two of my sheep back when I lived a humbler lifestyle," Ivette cut in.

Charles chuckled and shook his head, still refusing to speak about it. He'd been on an undercover assignment, blending in with rustlers. Unfortunately, he'd been caught by Ivette. But if he could keep his spy activities a secret as much as possible, then he would.

His friend continued, "It wasn't easy figuring it out. I had to do a little digging, and the Mother Goddess knows I was surprised when I uncovered your past." He wiped jam off his lip with a napkin. "I think most of the kingdom lives in unawares. But you clearly want to keep your identity a secret. You won't find us babbling."

"You are loyal friends," Charles murmured into his cup, taking a drink of his water to cover up his sentimentality. "You will find I am loyal to you as well."

And he meant far more than the mere loyalty of friendship. Although they didn't know it, they had his protection from the king in whatever capacity he was able to provide it. He'd learned years ago to never trust a king, not even your own. But it didn't mean he would refuse to work for one.

After a pause, Ivette asked, "You're going to fight for her, no?"

"She already gave me her answer."

"If you love someone, you can't give up on them." Ivette raised an eyebrow and stared pointedly at her husband. "Right, Barnaby?"

"Ah…" The other man ran a flustered hand over the back of his neck. "Uh huh. That's right. You'll never let me forget that, will you?"

She laughed. "Never."

Charles sat back in his chair and crossed his ankle over his knee, a frown a permanent fixture on his face. "She told me 'I can't.' What more can I do?"

"She can't *what?*" Barnaby lifted his brows. "Did she specify?"

"Can't marry me." His frown deepened. "I'm sure that's what she meant."

"Can't marry you? Or can't move away? Can't wait to marry you?"

"Can't right now for some unforeseen circumstance?" Ivette joined in. "Can't commit yet? Can't wait to commit?"

"Stop," he growled, turning away from them. "She made it abundantly clear that she wants to stay with her family and that I could never count as family. End of discussion."

A heavy pause.

And then…

"What's her name?" Ivette asked, motioning a servant inside the room and taking parchment and ink from him before he scampered back out. "We'll invite her for tea. You will happen to be invited, too. And the two of you can reconcile your differences and everything will work out as it should."

"Don't forget to invite her family," Barnaby added. "You will need to make a favorable impression."

Charles pointed to the two of them. "No wonder you attracted each other. You just can't stay out of anyone else's business."

They laughed before meeting in the middle for a short, sweet kiss. He looked away, staring out the window at the rain pouring down from the sky in sheets. Droplets of rain hit the window, creating a natural musical ensemble in tune with the crackling fire and whistling wind.

It reminded him of Emmaline and her wonderful performance.

He missed her.

He wished more than anything that she was there with him, snuggling within the cozy armchair in front of a warm hearth.

After her rejection, he'd fled too quickly, refusing to hear what she'd had to say. The hurt had been too heavy to bear. Was there any possible way he could fix this between them?

She'd kissed him after learning of his true identity and occupation. Surely, it didn't count for nothing.

"I'm not sure anyone would travel a good few hours for tea," he murmured against his palm resting on his chin.

The other two paused in their conversation before Ivette began scribbling excitedly on her parchment once again. "Oh, you would be surprised how far someone will travel to have tea with an earl." She elbowed Barnaby in the ribs. "And you certainly underestimate the lengths someone will go to for love."

"She doesn't love me."

"Are you so sure?"

His gaze flickered to the dancing flames as he held in a sigh. No, he wasn't sure at all. She had never told him she *didn't* love him. Then again, he hadn't exactly said the words, either. Perhaps things might have turned out differently if he had.

"What's the worst that can happen?" Ivette asked. "She'll say no and not come?"

"Umm…yes?" He scrubbed a hand over his face. He'd pushed himself to his limits these past couple of weeks and felt ready to drop. The thought of traveling even twenty minutes to his home fatigued his body beyond mention.

Ivette handed the parchment to her husband. "You have better handwriting. You write the invitation."

Barnaby shoved the writing materials into Charles' hands instead. "Better yet…"

"I'm not writing anything," he grumbled, shoving it right back.

"But you have rather princely handwriting." His friend pushed it away again.

"And you have rather earl-like handwriting." Charles shoved it back. And then his friend plucked the quill from his fingers and tickled the feather beneath his nose. "Gah!" Finally, he snatched the quill and the pad of parchment, scowling at Barnaby as he dipped the end of the quill into ink.

The last thing he wanted was to be humiliated again. But Ivette was right. He couldn't give up because Emmaline was worth fighting for.

"You'd better be paying for postage," Charles glowered as he scratched the quill against the parchment.

"I'll do you one better." Barnaby clapped him on the shoulder, nearly making him lose control of the quill. "I'll have my men hand deliver it themselves."

Chapter Fifteen

"**A**re you ready?" Oliver asked several days after Charles' departure, walking toward Emmaline while holding the reins of the horse in his hand. The creature was saddled and looked eager to begin another journey, even so soon after finishing the last one.

She wrapped her cloak more securely around herself to ward off the morning chill. She bit her lip and glanced down at her attire, uncertainty running rampant through her veins. A white shirt tucked into fitting, black leather trousers, the blouse dipping low enough to show a small amount of cleavage. A black leather vest lay snug against her over the blouse. The clothing was flattering to her figure. But… "I should have worn a dress."

"You rarely wear dresses." He waved away the notion with his hand. "Show the man the true Emmaline. Either he accepts you or he doesn't."

There were plenty of perks of being an outcast, and one of them was not conforming to the beauty standards placed on women in society. But suddenly she felt insecure, especially now knowing Charles to be a former prince, and he'd likely courted lovely women who wore dresses in the past. The best way to handle this was to ease into her true self.

Unfortunately, her brother was right. Either he accepted her, or he didn't.

Other members of her family waved at her and wished her good luck on her short journey to Edilann. She took a deep breath and placed her foot in the stirrup but paused at the sound of horses thundering down the path.

Her eyebrows furrowed as she stood beside Oliver and watched as men in matching blue and gold uniforms stormed into the clearing on horseback.

Fear raced through her, and she took a step closer to her brother. The color of the men's uniforms indicated they hailed from Edilann.

The soldier at the front glanced around at their party before honing in on her. He kicked his horse forward, stopping a few paces away. Oliver stepped in front of her as if to shield her, his hand resting on the pommel of his sword.

"Who are you?" Oliver asked in a gravelly tone.

The man briefly glanced his way before returning his attention to Emmaline. "I have come to deliver a letter for a Miss Emmaline Blythe."

"A letter?" Her eyebrows furrowed as she watched him reach into his breast pocket and pull out an envelope. "You don't look like a messenger."

He shook his head. "I am in the service of Earl Barnaby Mavis of Edilann."

She exchanged a confused look with her brother before she took the letter from the man and hesitantly broke the seal.

But then her heart pounded when she immediately recognized the handwriting. Her legs nearly collapsed beneath her, but somehow, she remained steady with the help of her mount beside her.

Hope fluttered in her chest as her gaze excitedly jumped across the page. Indeed, the letter was written in Charles' own handwriting.

Dear Emmaline,

I wanted to apologize for the way I left. I did not handle things as well as I should have, and I am deeply sorry if I hurt you. At the very least, I should have said goodbye rather than fled like the coward I am.

I hoped that, perhaps, you might give me a second chance. We can take this slower if you'd like. And if you wouldn't like, your friendship still means a great deal to me.

I hoped you and your family might join me and my friends for tea. The journey is not too long, and I would like to see you safe. Even if I have to coax you across the border with the promise of good food and wine. I mean, tea. All right, so I'm not much of a tea lover, but Barnaby insists it must be tea. I'll show you my wine cellar and we can sneak off with a vintage bottle for the special occasion of your visit.

Don't show this letter to Oliver. He'll have my head.

My heart and soul,
Charles, With Love

"Too late!" Oliver sang behind her, tapping the letter with his finger. "I already saw it. And yes, I'll have his head."

She ignored him while staring at the closing of the letter, all while her brother's words from earlier came to mind. *"Charles said the marriage was arranged. He never said the woman was his heart and soul."*

Although she knew how distraught he'd been over Lillian's death, and how tragic the event had been… She'd thought she'd need to compete for the special place in Charles's heart.

But…

My heart and soul.

She held the letter to her breast, uncaring that she had an audience as she did it. Perhaps she still had a chance to be that special person in his life.

"Who are Charles' friends?" she asked one of the soldiers when the overbearing warmth in her chest softened.

"Lord Barnaby Mavis, Lord Edward Beaumont, and Sir Tobie Lambton," he answered.

Her hand flew to her cheek. "Goodness!" Two of them were titled, and she feared asking just how far they ranked in terms of Edilann nobility. But what still scared her the most was Prince Christopher Avington.

He's not a prince anymore, she reminded herself, taking a steady breath to calm her racing heart. *And his name is now Charles.*

And then she put the pieces of the puzzle together. The soldier had said he worked for Barnaby Mavis. One of Charles' friends was an earl.

"I need to change my clothing."

But just as she attempted to race back toward her tent, Oliver grabbed her by the shoulder and pushed her toward the horse.

"You packed a dress," he reminded her. "If you must, you can change after our journey."

"We brought horses for you," the soldier gestured to two mounts with empty saddles.

Oliver answered. "We'll bring one of our own." He murmured under his breath, but she still heard it. "In case things go south."

"Are you expecting this to go so poorly?" she asked as she placed her foot in the stirrup and threw her other leg over the saddle.

"Knowing you?" He rolled his eyes and mounted the steed offered to him. "Absolutely."

She kicked him in the leg before spurring her horse forward to join the soldiers. She knew her brother was only jesting, but a part of her feared she might muck this up again a second time.

And more than anything, she hoped it would not be the case.

"We can kill her right now."

Poisoner clutched her wound and clenched her teeth, watching as the pretty little thing passed by below with an entourage of soldiers at her side. An arrow to the head would take her down quickly, but when she was wounded, escaping the guards unscathed was not an option.

"Yes, but then we'll never learn Huntsman's location." She chuckled under her breath, ignoring the excruciating pain consuming her abdomen. "I don't care what my orders are. This has become personal."

"So, we follow her?" her companion asked.

She nodded, glaring when the woman laughed at something one of the men said. "We follow her."

When the soldiers moved out of sight, she dropped down from the tree, stumbling to the side before catching herself against a branch. She didn't know where Huntsman lived, but she was sure she was about to find out.

Charles wiped his palms on his trousers and fanned air into his shirt. Flashes of warmth attacked his body as he stared at himself in the mirror. He'd changed his clothing three times. Normally, he wasn't one to care overly much about his appearance, but he feared one wrong move might scare Emmaline away.

Emmaline, who would arrive within the hour.

And then in a couple days, he would meet with the king. He still didn't know what he was going to tell him about the Leonian princess. He didn't want an innocent young woman to die over throne wars, and he feared telling him the truth might put Emmaline in danger, too.

Barnaby entered the room without knocking, gave him a once over, and sighed. "That color doesn't go with those pants."

The other man shut the door behind him, smoothed down his already neat blond hair, and flicked a thread off his black coat. He always dressed impeccably, with clothes tailored to fit him perfectly. Nothing out of place. He always had women fawning over him right and left. It was any wonder he'd settled down with Ivette at all.

Well, not that he'd had much choice. Edilann law forced the nobility to marry by age twenty-four. It was simply lucky he'd met the right person at the right time.

His friend threw a light blue tunic at him, and while he grumpily changed *again*, Barnaby dug through his armoire, placing items neatly back where they'd come from until he found a pair of brown boots and tossed them next.

Charles huffed. "Not those. I don't think Emma likes it when I look…princely."

Barnaby grinned from ear to ear. "Then we'll make you look a bit slovenly. Like a lazy prince."

"That's worse."

"I promise you, it's not. She'll fall flat on her face in love."

"What do you know?"

His friend looked at him pointedly. "If I know anything, it's fashion. And the outfits you have chosen look atrocious."

Charles huffed, throwing his previous clothing choice at Barnaby's face before changing into the entire ensemble. He looked at himself in the mirror again and glared. To his annoyance, he looked good. But he wasn't about to admit it.

Taking a step forward, Barnaby mussed up his hair and unfastened the top button of his shirt. Next, he instructed him to roll his sleeves halfway up his arms.

"I hate this," he grumbled.

"Are you trying to get the girl or what?"

"I can do it just fine on my own."

Barnaby raised an eyebrow. "You already managed to muddle it up once. You need help, Charles."

Unfortunately, he was right. He was terrible at courting. He never knew the right thing to say. His quiet demeanor often turned people away. He always managed to offend when he was trying to flirt.

His friend attempted to hand him a vest next, but he batted it away. He was done playing dress up. A man could only take so much fussing before he went insane.

A servant knocked, his voice muffled through the door. "Miss Emmaline has arrived at the end of the drive."

"Dear goddess," Charles gasped, his hand flying to his heart when it squeezed a bit too hard in his chest. "She actually came."

He quickly strapped on his thigh-holster daggers, much to Barnaby's lamenting about ruining his outfit, tied a sword to his belt, and tucked several knives on his person before he rushed out of the room, across the hallway, and down the flight of stairs of his home. He only kept one servant, an old, loyal friend to the king, as Godfrey knew who he really was and what he did for a living.

Godfrey opened the front door of his estate, where his three other friends and Ivette joined him. The five of them stood on the drive, watching as an entourage of soldiers escorted two people on horseback.

The sight of blonde curls stole his breath away, followed by an anxious squeeze to his chest. Emmaline rode with confident magnificence on top of her steed, her curls bouncing with the gait of the horse. She steered the creature with elegance in each of her movements, her posture straight and poised.

His heart beat in tandem with the horse's hooves, speeding up only when she neared enough for a clearer view of her beautiful face and captivating blue eyes.

Edward gaped beside him. "Is that her?"

"Is she wearing trousers?" Tobie gasped quietly.

Barnaby laughed and clapped him on the shoulder, ignoring his scowl. "Oh, she is perfect for you. I can already see it. I think I may have wasted my efforts on making you look presentable. She probably won't care."

"Barnaby!" Ivette scolded. "That was insensitive. She is lovely."

"I never said she wasn't. She's a dream. But please. Trousers? She's Charles' perfect match."

Several paces away, Emmaline reined back her horse before dismounting, standing before him with a look of defiance in her eyes. She held her head high as if awaiting his judgment on her choice of clothing. But all he managed to do was flush from his neck to his ears. She looked…incredible. The trousers suited her. And her blouse…

His neck heated when he realized just how low the front dipped, the white fabric loose around the shoulders but tucked into her trousers to give her a slender but curvy in the right places kind of look.

Realizing he was staring, his gaze jumped back to her face to find her features had softened, replaced by a stirring warmth.

"Charles," she murmured.

He stuffed his hands into his pockets. "Hi, Emma." But then he grunted when Barnaby elbowed him in the ribs. Quickly, he unstuffed his hands and offered her his arm.

Although she seemed to try to hide it, he couldn't help but notice how her fingers shook as she linked her arm with his. His soul could have cried out with joy.

Because it felt as if she'd come home.

"Allow me to introduce my friends," he continued, gesturing to each one. "Barnaby and his wife, Ivette. Tobie. And Edward. Everyone, this is Emma and her brother, Oliver."

Oliver lifted a hand in greeting beside them.

"Oh, you are lovely!" Ivette exclaimed, stealing Emmaline from him, much to his dismay. "How tired you must be from your journey. Come on inside. Charles' home is rather beautiful. The best view is from the drawing room."

Emmaline stopped at the garden to admire the variety of flowers, trailing her fingers along the petals of pink peonies. A smile lifted on her lips when several birds flapped down and splashed into the bird bath, and then her appreciative gaze took in the entirety of the house.

He silently thanked Godfrey for the upkeep of the estate, as his line of work often took him away for periods of time. He wanted Emmaline to like it here. It was…peaceful.

But then he glared when he found Tobie and Edward still staring after her as she disappeared inside with the others.

"Stop looking at her backside," Charles hissed, squeezing Tobie's shoulder. Hard.

"How can I not? It's right *there*. Besides, I know you're looking, too."

"I rather like her trousers look. But keep your eyes up. Got it?"

Both nodded and started toward the house. He frowned as he followed after, panic consuming him when he suddenly forgot everything Barnaby had gone over with him. What to say. How to say it. What to do. What not to do. On the road, he hadn't needed to know those things. Keeping Emmaline safe had been his priority, and things had fallen into place around him. But now? He needed to impress her, and he hadn't the slightest idea how.

When he entered the drawing room to join the others, everyone glanced his way before the room burst into laughter. "What's so funny?" Was it his hair? His clothing? He knew he should have forsaken the boots.

Barnaby snorted. "Emmaline here made a wager that you would scowl within the first minute, and here you are, walking into the room scowling."

They laughed again. His gaze darted to Emmaline who wore a playful smirk on her pretty pink lips. She sat on the settee with her legs crossed, looking comfortable where she lounged on the light blue furniture. The space beside her lay empty, as if his friends had purposefully seated him beside her.

"Are you done laughing at my expense?" he asked as he took the cup of tea Godfrey offered him. He sipped on the hot liquid where he stood and grimaced. How anyone drank tea was beyond him. It was disgusting.

Laughter rose up again, and this time he glowered at everyone in the room. "What now?"

Oliver answered with a knowing look, "I took a wager you would gag on your tea. You'd better find your wine stash, eh?"

His gaze jumped to Emmaline, only to find her grimacing. She blushed and mouthed, *Sorry*.

It seemed her brother had read the letter he'd sent her. It was too late to feign ignorance.

"Come now," Ivette said with a grin. "You know we love you. Now take a seat. Hovering in the doorway is bad luck."

Uncertainty ran rampant through his blood, followed by an anxious churn of his stomach. He'd faced plenty of social outings with nobility. Even the assignments the king gave him never scared him. But none of those things had involved his heart.

"You have a beautiful home, Charles." Emmaline offered him a smile, and suddenly he realized why he felt so…unsettled. He didn't like idle chit chat. He liked tackling the root of the problem without the constraints of social frivolity.

"Would you like a tour?"

"Right now?"

He nodded. "Right now."

Oliver pointed at the two of them as Emmaline stood to join him at the door. "No bedrooms or broom closets. I'm warning you."

Emmaline rolled her eyes as she took Charles' arm. "Don't forget, dear brother, that I am older than you."

"And I am taller than you."

When her back was turned, Barnaby gave him an encouraging thumbs up. It didn't help much to calm his anxious nerves.

Rather than focusing on the nervous tension in each of his muscles, he showed her around the main floor from the kitchen to the dining room and everything in between. As she ran her fingers over the frame holding a painting of the landscape outside his home, she turned to look at him over her shoulder.

"So…you have titled friends," she began hesitantly, eyes glancing down the hallway where the drawing room resided.

"Uhh…yeah." He scratched his jaw. "I suppose this is the life I am accustomed to and the kind of people I'm more familiar with."

She continued her exploration by opening closets and gazing out a window overlooking the garden. "I feel underdressed for the occasion."

"Occasion?" He snorted. "Having tea is not the most exciting occasion I can think of. Besides, it's just my friends. They're actually quite nice."

"And nonjudgmental?"

"And what?" Then he realized she was speaking about her choice of clothing. "Well, it did come a bit as a surprise. But I like it."

"This is how I dress when I'm not wearing stolen princess gowns. Most of the time."

Unable to help himself, he laughed as he guided her farther down the hallway. "Don't think I didn't see you stripped down to stockings and a corset during your performance. I was more shocked then than I was when you arrived wearing trousers."

They passed the main bedroom, and he inhaled sharply as he reached for the double doors and shut them. "Oh, sorry. No bedrooms."

She shook her head and laughed as she tightened her grip on his arm. "You shared a bedroll with me for quite a few nights. I think a bedroom tour is the least of our worries." She turned the handles and pushed. The doors swung back open to reveal light flooding in from the windows, illuminating a large, canopied bed with a subtle floral bedspread. A writing desk rested against the wall in front of one of the windows, and the other boasted a window seat with soft, floral cushions.

"This is your room?" she asked with awe in her voice, and as she turned in a full circle to admire her surroundings, the sunlight caught onto her hair and stole his breath. He loved her blonde hair. It made her look…angelic.

"No." He cleared his throat and leaned against the doorframe, not wanting to betray Oliver's trust by stepping inside with her. "Well, perhaps one day when I marry again. But my room is upstairs. I prefer being able to see all my property." He shrugged. "You know, in case there are unwanted visitors."

"And have there been?"

Once again, he shrugged to try to hide the anxiety stirring in his chest. "A family of black bears. A few raccoons. Deer chomped on my garden. But I don't consider them unwelcome."

"Can I have this room?"

He lifted his eyebrows, his heart skipping in his chest. "Come again?"

A sultry grin lifted on her lips, more teasing than anything. "I assume Oliver and I will be staying here for the night, unless you want us to rent a couple rooms in the city."

He released a long breath. "I hadn't thought that far. I…" He ran a hand over the back of his neck. "I didn't think you'd come."

She threw her head back and laughed, the sound striking him straight through the heart like an arrow hitting its target.

"I was already on my way when I got your letter. Oliver *really* wanted to finish that game."

"And what about you?"

"I *really* wanted to watch you beat him for real this time."

His lips parted in surprise, words fleeing from him entirely as he watched her move past him into the hallway. By the time she reached the back door leading to the garden and helped herself outside, his wits finally returned to him, and he found himself scrambling after her.

The moment he stepped outside, he blinked back the bright light of late afternoon, his eyes trying to adjust as he searched for Emmaline in the yard. He found her admiring the flowers tucked up against the side of the house before she ventured across the green lawn toward the apple tree on his property.

Juicy and red. Filled with sweet promises, love, and laughter. In his culture, apples had symbolized happiness. So, he'd planted the tree on his property and watched as it grew over the years into what it was now.

Charles ran a hand over his jaw as he approached her hesitantly beneath the apple tree. He still didn't know where he stood, and his awkward self was trying to figure out how to ask.

But before he managed to speak, she spun around to face him and beat him to it.

"I wanted to apologize."

He furrowed his brows, suddenly feeling lost. "What do *you* have to apologize for? You've done nothing wrong."

A huff escaped her as she threw her hands up. "You scared me, Charles. When I put on that gown, I was ready for you.

For a life with you. But when you showed up looking like the prince you were, it terrified me."

He frowned at his offending boots. "I knew you didn't like it when I dressed this way."

"You misunderstand me. I love it. It suits you. It looks good on you. But it made me realize…" Her voice cracked.

Softening his tone, he asked, "Realize what?"

"What if I'm no good for you?" She ran a strand of her curly hair through her fingers. "In another life, you wouldn't have turned your eye toward me. I'm not…I'm not exactly nobility material. I'm not sure I can fit in with your lifestyle and the people who surround you."

"Emma." He took both her hands and held them to his heart. "In another life, I had no choice in the matter. In this life, I do. You are what I want. You are what I think is good for me. And who cares what others think? My friends accept you. It's all you need if you want a place in court."

She laughed dryly but didn't retract her hands from his. "Just look at Ivette! She makes such a beautiful, charming countess. I cannot compete with that."

His eyes widened as he dropped her hands. The situation was so unbearably funny that he couldn't help himself from snorting and then laughing into his hand to attempt to hide it. But hard as he tried, the sound escaped as an uncontrollable guffaw.

Emmaline planted her hands on her hips. "I don't think this is amusing."

"Oh, no. It's very amusing." He gestured toward the house, still chuckling. "You truly have no idea who Ivette is. She was a sheep girl who lived on a sheep farm, taking care of her four sisters by herself. No money. No title. Nothing.

Barnaby fell in love with her and that was the end of that." He took her gently by the shoulders. "You think you can't fit in with them? You'd be surprised at just how well you already do."

"Even though I wear trousers?" She chuckled weakly as she wiped a tear from her cheek.

"Especially then."

Another tear wipe. "I can't leave my family behind. I love performing with them."

"Do you perform year-round?"

"Well…no. Mostly during the summers."

He nodded, plans formulating in his mind. Sacrificing time with her would not be easy, but he'd do anything to make this work. If he could only convince her… "Then we will see each other sporadically during the summers and spend the rest of the time here in Edilann. I go on special *trips* now and again, but I'm never usually gone more than a few weeks."

"Charles," she breathed, now holding tight to his hands while hope flickered in her eyes.

Oh, he was terrible at reading her cues. He didn't want to propose again, only to get shot down. Did she need more convincing? He only held one more card, but if it didn't work…

He had nothing left.

"You have the most beautiful voice," he murmured, brushing his thumb along the back of her hand. "I can give you the opportunity to sing for royalty. To perform at balls and weddings and dinner parties. I don't like the idea of fighting off your admirers, but I will if I must."

She blinked rapidly as she released a shaky breath. "Charles…"

But as he gazed back into her watery eyes, he realized he *did* have one more card to play. It was a terrifying card. One he didn't want to relinquish. Because it would leave him far too vulnerable for comfort.

However, he would do anything to keep her.

So, he laid his last card down.

"I love you, Emma."

Emmaline squeezed her eyes shut, and tears escaped either side and ran down her cheeks. "Several weeks ago, you would never have said those words. You hated me."

"But you weren't *you*, were you?"

"I suppose not," she laughed in a watery tone. She placed one hand on his waist and the other on his chest. "I love it here, Charles. I love this house. I really like your friends. But most of all…I love you. If you truly believe we can make this work, then let's make this work."

He released a long breath, expelling the anxious tension from his body. "I want you to believe it can, too."

"I do. I don't want to be without you. It was hard enough to last even a day of your absence."

Charles ran a hand over his jaw to try to disguise the emotion gripping him hard. He'd never thought he'd marry again. He'd never imagined he would get a second chance, for someone else to allow him to love them and protect them and cherish them.

Therefore, he had no words as he reached into his pocket and pulled out a gold ring with light-blue, pear-shaped gemstones. "I thought the color matched your eyes," he finally managed in a raspy tone.

He slipped the ring onto her finger and watched as she admired how the gems sparkled in the sunlight. When she turned back to him, her face radiated sunshine and happiness, mirroring the elation he felt inside.

"No third-party negotiator needed," she teased with a poke to his ribs.

Shaking his head in a self-deprecating manner, he replied, "Then you are not aware of just how much weight Barnaby had to pull to get me this far."

Her laughter warmed his entire body with the sweet, melodic sound. "Then you must thank him for the both of us." She surprised him by grabbing his shirt and pulling him down for a kiss. He melted into her, his hands naturally finding their place at her waist as if he'd known her far longer than he had.

After six long years, he was finally home.

Emmaline laughed as she broke away and glanced down at her attire. "Now I feel very underdressed for the occasion. I knew I should have changed."

He smiled as joy filled his entire being. He leaned closer and murmured in her ear. "I love you just the way you are."

And then he pulled her in for another kiss when simply holding her at the waist wasn't enough.

The sound of a window creaking open reached his ears, followed by Oliver's voice, irritating in the moment. "Oi! I said no kissing!"

Charles heaved a long sigh as he pulled away from his new intended. Oliver truly seemed determined to get Emmaline to the altar untouched. But it was not in his nature to break even his own rules. He would always treat her like a gentleman ought to.

Of course, Emmaline lifted her head defiantly and fisted her hands at her hips. "No, you said no broom closets. The outdoors is fair game."

Oliver perked up, leaning precariously out the window. "What's that? Is that a ring? Are you two engaged?"

An excited clamor sounded from within the house, becoming louder when Emmaline held up her hand to display the ring to her brother.

His friends rushed outside to see the ring and to congratulate them. Fluster burned his face, and he lifted his hand to his mouth to try to hide it as they gave him pats on the back and punches to the shoulder. Ivette tightly embraced the both of them. A part of him wanted to escape. To flee from the attention. But another part of him wanted to show off his new fiancée when the elation of happiness burned bright in his soul.

Oliver clapped him on the shoulder. "I suppose this means we need to finish that game tonight."

Emmaline gave his hand a reassuring squeeze, and he found the courage to nod. "I hope you are prepared to lose."

Chapter Sixteen

There was a reason engagements were often short. Because all Charles wanted was to spend every waking moment with Emmaline. To hold her close. To kiss her. To spend the night with her in his arms and wake up to her beautiful smile in the morning. He'd taken the time on the road with her for granted, and he only wished he'd had the sense to better appreciate the time they'd had together.

A smile pulled up on his lips as he climbed the wooden staircase leading to the second story of his home, a lantern in his hands to light the way.

He could hardly believe it. He was an engaged man. And the lovely woman in question was staying downstairs in his home.

Elation burned bright in his soul. When he'd left the troupe, he'd never thought he would see Emmaline again, let alone find himself engaged to her. He was ever grateful to Barnaby for knocking sense back into him. He would have lost so much should he have given up.

Oliver passed him on the staircase, doing a fancy card trick by tossing the cards smoothly from one hand to the other. "See you downstairs. You're going to have to work real hard to win, Charles. Prepare to play all night."

He smirked. "I don't plan on it taking that long at all."

He jogged up the rest of the staircase and used a key to unlock the door to his room with the intent to grab a sand timer for the occasion. He closed the door behind him, grimacing when he realized he didn't want anyone peeking their heads inside. Not only did he hide valuable information in strategic places, but weapons of every size and shape lay scattered about.

He didn't want Emmaline knowing he was a weapon hoarder. At least not yet.

Swords rested side by side on a wall mount. Daggers lay in sheaths across one of the short, rectangular bookshelves housing books about law, edible plants in nature, and everything in between. Another rack held several bows while a few quivers of arrows rested against the wall in the corner.

A bowl of vivid red apples on his writing desk drew his attention. Red and ripe and recently picked from the looks of it. Godfrey spoiled him far more than he deserved.

Next to the apples lay a stack of letters, and he sifted through them for anything important. He found a few "courtesy" social invites that he only sometimes attended when he thought he might glean valuable information from such outings. Another letter from the palace sparked his interest.

He absently reached for an apple and bit through the juicy flesh before he broke the seal on the envelope and poured over information about the latest trades and stocks. Thankfully, his "job" as a trader fascinated him, making it much easier to keep up the ruse, especially in court. He knew the inside and out of his supposed trade and did a convincing job at upholding his identity.

An overbearing itch climbed his throat, and he cleared it to try to expel the scratchy sensation. It broke him out of his thoughts and pulled him back to the present. He set the letter down and took another bite of the apple as he opened one of the drawers in his desk and pulled out an hourglass.

He scratched the outside of his throat and coughed when the itch refused to abate. Water. He needed water.

Thankfully, his waterskin from his journey was still halfway full where it rested on the chair in front of his writing desk. Bringing it to his lips, he took a long swig but spat half of it out when he began choking on the water when swallowing proved difficult.

He dropped the waterskin, liquid splashing across the bottom of his shoes. Next went his hourglass, glass shattering and sand spilling across the wooden floors. Raspy breaths struggled to enter his lungs with every inhale, and for a moment, he thought a piece of apple might have lodged in his throat.

His lungs panicked, aching for air. He pounded on his chest and coughed some more. But then his eyes widened as foamy spittle flew from his mouth.

Poison.

He'd been poisoned.

The apple in his hand dropped to the ground, rolling across the floor. He gasped for each breath as he drew his sword and spun around to find Poisoner standing in front of the door. A smirk grew across her face as she turned the lock.

"I've leveled the playing field," she said, drawing her own weapon, but not without a wince of pain. "Let's see how well you fare now."

Charles swiped at the woman, but when his head spun and his lungs seized, he lost his balance and stumbled into the swing. Poisoner caught her blade against his and kicked the back of his knee. He crashed into the bookcase. Books spilled across the floor. Weapons clattered deafeningly against the ground.

Breaths heaved in and out of his lungs. He choked on poisonous spittle. He gasped for air.

He tried to call out a warning to the others downstairs, but all that escaped was a choked gurgle.

Poisoner grabbed his arm and shoved him into the writing desk. Wooden legs snapped. The desk crashed onto its side. The chair toppled on top of him.

The woman grabbed the chair and smashed it right above him. Wood shattered. Splintered pieces rained over his head. His fingers fumbled for one of his daggers strapped to his thigh. He barely managed to unsheathe it before she stepped on his hand. A cry of pain escaped him. Someone pounded on the door. But he could do nothing more than choke on foamy spittle as his body began spasming.

The airways to his lungs became blocked by fluid. He choked again, coughing and spluttering as he tried to fight through the spasms. But his body refused to obey him.

The door creaked and shuttered as if the person on the other side tried to break it down. He wanted to call out for them to stop. To flee. But darkness slowly seeped into his vision. His body ceased spasming. His lungs gave up the fight for air.

And his world turned dark.

"Charles!" Emmaline screeched, pounding on his bedroom door with both fists. Items crashed from within. She heard more than one pair of footsteps inside, followed by a female voice. Charles was in danger.

Why didn't he answer? Why didn't he answer!

"Move aside," Oliver ordered. With one strong kick, the door splintered the slightest bit near his foot. The second kick splintered the wood by the doorknob. The third kick broke the door from the lock, and it flew open and crashed against the wall inside the room.

Emmaline's hand flew to her mouth at the chaos within. Broken wood lay scattered about the room. A series of weapons were sprawled across the ground, mixed with sand and glass. The window shutters bounced with the wind on the opposite side of the room, and without a care for herself, she sprinted to the window and peered out, only to find darkness.

But then she spotted a flicker of white below.

Her stomach twisted.

One horse disappeared into the trees, the rider holding the reins, and another limp body draped over the creature's back in front of them. The second person on horseback turned with a wicked grin on her face.

"I'll have fun hunting you next!" Poisoner cackled before spurring her mount after the other until she, too, disappeared into the darkness.

Quick, raspy breaths heaved in and out of her lungs as she stared disbelieving at the place the woman had disappeared. Charles. She took Charles. But alive or dead?

She stumbled backward, tripping over something on the ground. She cried out in alarm, bracing herself for impact. But her brother caught her before she hit the floor.

"Be calm," Oliver murmured as he pulled her close and rubbed her back soothingly as she cried. "Be calm. Be calm."

"I can't. I can't!"

On the edge of hysterics, her hands shook as her brother sat her down on the bed and rummaged about the room. Nothing added up. Charles hadn't been upstairs for long. Why hadn't he called for help? He would have at least said *something*. Clearly, a fight had happened in this room. But it had sounded more like a beating than a fight.

She'd seen Charles in action. He was not one to be beaten so easily. Nor one to be taken off guard.

"Emma," Oliver murmured with despair in his tone as he held up a red apple by the stem. Two bites had been taken out of the fruit, but no more.

"What does that have to do with anything? We need to go after him!"

"It was eaten recently," he explained. Next, he picked up the sword Charles always carried on his person and turned it around to inspect it. "No dents or scratches. He didn't use it."

Her eyes flashed open when she finally understood. Poisoner had come after Charles. From what he had told Emmaline, Poisoner hadn't known who Charles truly was nor where he lived.

"She followed us here," she gasped. "We put him in danger."

"Emma," he said again in a soft, placating tone, holding up the apple once again.

The blood drained from her face. For a moment, it felt as if her heart ceased beating. The apple didn't look normal. Small drips of liquid rolled down the fruit and plopped onto the floor. A regular apple wouldn't behave in such a manner.

"He was poisoned."

She covered her face with her hands as she tried to hold the panic at bay and think with a clear head. It wasn't easy when she wanted to scream out in heartache. She only just got Charles back. Losing him now would destroy her.

"Why would they have taken him if he were dead?" she asked in a miserable tone.

"They wouldn't have," he answered, setting the apple down with the rest of the fruit in the bowl on the desk. He heaved a sigh and turned to her with a guilty expression. "I overheard your conversation with him in the tent. And before you get angry at me, I eavesdropped because I needed to make sure you were safe with him. I promise you, everything he told you will never leave my lips."

"Then you know what he does for a living."

Oliver nodded. "If they took him alive… Emma, they will torture him for information. He won't stay alive for long."

She swiped enraged tears from her eyes. She was angry. At the world for betraying him again and again. At herself for leading the enemy to his doorstep. At Poisoner for hurting the man she loved with her entire heart.

She stood and crossed the room toward Charles' enormous collection of daggers and began strapping several to her person. She didn't know how to wield a sword nor how to shoot a bow. But daggers were something she thought she could handle.

"Don't think you're going alone." He, too, took a sword and several knives from Charles' outrageous hoard of weapons. "I'm coming with you."

Gratitude swelled within her chest as she rushed downstairs with her brother at her heels. Determination fueled her actions as she strode toward the bag she'd left in the room she was staying in.

"Just let me grab my makeup."

Chapter Seventeen

A weight sat on Charles' chest. Heavy. Suffocating. His lungs burned. His head screamed with agony. He tried to breathe, but he inhaled fluid, choking and spluttering in his desperate attempts for air.

Finally, his eyes flashed open. But immediately, his surroundings spun, preventing him from grasping onto an image long enough to make sense of it.

His next attempt to push himself to sitting only managed to shove more water into his face. He coughed, gasping for each breath until his lungs ceased their seizing. Air wheezed in and out of his lungs as he noticed his damp clothing and his soaked hair clinging to his face and neck.

Where was he?

Panicked breaths fogged up the glass only a few finger lengths away from his face. To his horror, he found another wall of glass on either side of him, boxing him in like a tub with a glass ceiling.

He pounded on the glass overhead, but it held steady as if it were thick and impenetrable. Another wave of panic clawed at his chest as he attempted to kick out the bottom of the glass tub. But when he had no room to move, he couldn't get the leverage needed to free himself.

Water lapped at his shoulders, the chill seeping straight through his clothing and into his bones. His teeth chattered. His limbs shivered. His mind felt sluggish as if trudging through thick mud.

Where was he? How had he gotten here?

"A double dose of poison took longer to wear off, unfortunately."

Charles inhaled sharply at the sound of the familiar voice entering the glass through several small holes in the top of the rigid structure. He swiped his wet arm across the glass to his right, leaving a watery streak in his wake. His heart leaped to his throat when he found Poisoner casually leaning against the wall with arms crossed as she stared at him, as if she'd been watching him for some time now.

"What have you done?" he growled, but the sound escaped more like a pathetic rasp when his throat burned, and each breath he drew was agony.

The woman flipped her short black hair out of her face. Glass vials filled with ranging colors of liquid clacked in her hands as she shifted them around her fingers. "The Huntsman became the hunted."

Through his foggy mind, memories flashed before him. Eating the apple. Getting poisoned. Trying but failing to fight back. The rest was a blur of black and pain.

"You could have done away with me anytime you wanted," he croaked. "Why am I still alive?"

She tsked. "Oh, *Charles*." A grin spread across her face at using his real name. "I want what you have in here." She tapped the side of her head. "Number one rule of being a spy—don't get caught."

He hacked up more fluid in his lungs, realizing the poison from earlier still moved through his body. He felt weak and vulnerable, void of the strength and vitality once coursing through his blood.

"What could I possibly give you?" he choked, his voice echoing through the glass tub—no, not a tub.

A coffin.

Glass vials clacked together again as she pushed away from the wall and slowly approached, her voice muffled through the coffin. "Nothing on Edilann, to be sure. As I understand it…you have a great deal of information about Armandy. I want what you gave King Royce."

He internally cursed. "The information is not for sale."

"Oh, I never intended to *buy* it." She tipped her head to the side to study him. "You know how much I enjoy torturing information out of my sources. And…" She leaned her arms against the coffin and stared down at him. "If you don't comply, I will torture your fair little maiden next."

Icy fear crawled up his spine as he stared at the bottomless pit of cruelty in her eyes, distorted through the foggy glass. If she laid a single hand on Emmaline, he would show no mercy.

"You're bluffing."

"Am I?" A malicious smirk stared him down. "Once you were down, the girl was ripe for the picking."

"Show her to me then."

She chuckled darkly. "That can be arranged. But currently, she's safe in her cell. There's no telling what would happen once my men fetch her."

Charles' nostrils flared as he searched for the lie in her eyes but didn't find anything but joy in others' pain. "Please, let her go. She is innocent in this."

"I will." She uncorked a vial with red liquid inside. "As soon as you give me everything I desire."

She poured the red liquid through the holes in the glass coffin. He hurried to squeeze his eyes shut and turn his head to the side, but the poison still splashed across his face, entering his nose and the corner of his mouth.

The fumes of the substance caused him to cough, which allowed more of the liquid to enter his mouth. His heart raced with panic. He kicked at the bottom of the glass coffin to no avail, water splashing across his face. Dark, terrifying images flashed before his eyes. His mind shrieked with terror. And when his throat burned as if with fire, he screamed.

"Now…" Poisoner leered down at him. "Tell me what I want to know."

Chapter Eighteen

This will never work, Emmaline couldn't help but think to herself as she crept along the outside of a gated property through the darkness. The house was more like a fortress with its imposing gray bricks and braziers blazing with yellow and orange flames.

Two male guards patrolled the grounds, armed with swords and adorned in gold, metallic armor. But after spending weeks in the royal palace, she immediately sensed something wasn't quite right with them. They wore palace uniforms, true. But their form, posture, and the weapons they carried led her to believe they were hired mercenaries.

Men who could be bought.

Perhaps Poisoner wasn't on any king's side at all. She only served her own interests.

Oliver motioned for her to stop in front of a large bush at the bend in the property. The gates were open, but that wasn't what concerned her.

She grimaced and placed a silver-armored hand over her heart as she imagined herself getting stabbed through the chest when the guards realized she wasn't who she said she was. She didn't want to die tonight. But she knew she needed to risk everything for the man who was likely getting tortured inside.

Taking a deep breath, she steeled her nerves and traded her fear for courage. Although she felt inadequate for what she must do tonight, Charles had no one else but them.

The seven dwarves stopped behind them. They had camped out a short distance from Charles' estate, too shy to meet his friends but not wanting to be far at the same time. Bear sidled up to her on nimble feet. He shook a vial, his eyebrows drawn with worry.

"Are you sure this antidote will work?" she asked quietly.

"Positive." He unwrapped the poisonous apple from Charles' room and held it carefully within the white cloth. Beneath the dull light of the full moon, he studied the contents of the vial next to the apple, looking for what, she didn't know. "This is a common poison used to subdue rather than kill. Charles is alive." She breathed a sigh of relief. At least until he added, "For now."

She hated those two words. Time was of the essence. Yet, there couldn't possibly be enough time in the world to save him from such a terrible fate.

She voiced her fears as she tucked the vial into her pocket. "If we're caught, Poisoner will take the vial from me."

Bear shook his head. "Oh, she'll likely search your person if you're caught, but she won't suspect it to be on your lips. Just a smudge will do the trick. It won't be harmful to you. But should he need it…"

The dwarf smeared the liquid substance across her lips. It tasted both sweet and bitter. Like berries mixed with tree sap. But she endured the taste when it gave her hope.

"Don't I get some, too?" Oliver asked with a mock pout.

She rolled her eyes and pinched his arm. "This is not the time, Ollie."

But then she glanced at the guards through the barbed bushes to make sure no one heard their hushed conversation. However, when she returned her attention to her brother, she found him staring at her.

"Are you sure you can do this?" he asked.

Her fingers hovered over the makeup on her face. Close but not touching. Mud coated her hair to make it look darker, the only thing available on such short notice. And her face…

She'd made herself take on Poisoner's exact appearance.

The voice would not be easy to replicate. The other woman had a deeper voice while Emmaline's was lighter and airier. But…

"What other choice do we have?" she murmured back. "We don't know how many men she has stationed on the inside."

"You're going to get yourself killed."

"What choice do I have?" she repeated, her voice cracking. "I would die for that man." Closing her eyes, she took a deep breath to steel her emotions. She needed a level head if she wanted to succeed tonight. "I can do this."

After a pause, Oliver nodded. "I know you can. The rest of us will find another way in."

She took a long look at her family members surrounding her. Memorizing their faces. Treasuring their loyalty.

And then she stood and strode confidently around the corner of the gate. She lengthened her stride to imitate Poisoner and casually rested an armored hand on the handle of her dagger.

The guards stationed near the door stood straighter as she approached, a snarl on her face. "I told you!" she hissed at the men in a deeper voice that she could barely manage. "Stay alert. I had to take care of a few lurkers myself. Do. Your. Job!"

"Yes, Ma'am," they both said in unison.

When she waved her hand, they stepped aside to let her in the front door. She braced herself for the sharp sting of a blade, but it never came. The mercenaries didn't look twice at her. For if they did, they might have noticed her hair was not as dark as she wished it were, and she wasn't quite as tall and muscular as their employer.

As she stepped inside, she had to hold back a cough at the ill-kept, dusty interior of the small fortress. The stone floor looked as if it hadn't been swept in ages. The torchlight flickering across stone walls illuminated a place bereft of decoration and furnishings.

Emmaline's heart pounded as she continued her long stride down the dank hallway, which opened into a larger room with a couple chairs circling a fire pit located in the ground. A man sat in one of the chairs, his feet propped up and his head lolling to the side as he slept.

The thought of killing anyone, especially while they were vulnerable, twisted her stomach with discomfort. If she could avoid such a thing *and* help clear the way for her family, then she would do it.

Without taking a moment to hesitate, she kicked the mercenary's legs so his feet fell to the ground with a thump. The man startled upright. Metal sang as he started to draw his sword but quickly stopped at the sight of her.

She scowled, glaring down at him. "Sleeping on the job? You're fired. Get out."

"But—"

"Get out, I said." She reached for her weapon, and the simple action had the man scrambling to his feet and rushing toward the exit.

A blood-curdling scream echoing from up the stone staircase to her right smashed into her heart and ripped it to shreds. It was muffled as if escaping from behind a closed door.

Charles! her mind screeched.

But the sound of shouts outside and weapon clashing against weapon reminded her to remain calm. Getting to Charles late was better than getting to him never.

Therefore, she leisurely walked out of the room and down the hallway, only to find a female mercenary rushing in her direction with her sword held at the ready. Every fiber of her being screamed at her to run. To flee. Perhaps even to fight.

But she allowed her disguise to work for her and feigned indifference.

"There's a disturbance outside," the woman gasped. "An attack on the perimeter of the fortress."

Wearing a look of boredom she'd seen on Poisoner's face before, Emmaline gestured down the hallway, indicating for the mercenary to look into it.

Without a backward glance, the mercenary did as instructed.

Her eyebrows furrowed, her heart beating hard in her chest as she crept down the darkened hallway. By the way Charles had screamed, everyone had to know Poisoner was with him rather than traversing the fortress corridors.

Unless she wasn't…

Emmaline quickened her pace when Charles screamed again, this time closer. Her calm demeanor broke at the torturous sound, and unable to help herself, she started running.

Someone shouted for her to stop down another hallway to her left. She kept going. Her breaths became ragged beneath all the armor she wore, beneath the weapons and heavy protection weighing down each step, until she turned around a sharp corner and crashed into the wall with the momentum.

A pained breath shuddered from her lungs as she limped forward. The sound of pursuit echoed closer, each clank of metal echoing down the stony corridor.

She drew her dagger and spun around. The man pursuing her stopped in his tracks, confusion furrowed in his brows.

Drat it all!

She remembered his face. He had been the only survivor aside from Poisoner after Charles had been ambushed in the forest. He'd seen her face before. Or rather, her eyes. They were a distinctive blue whereas Poisoner possessed a darker hue.

Her eyelids shuttered halfway closed to cast shadows over the color. But an even bigger problem remained.

He knew the sound of her voice. If she spoke, she would not survive.

Emmaline tried waving the man away, but he refused to budge.

The man moved closer. Panic raced through her hammering pulse as she backed away, trying to find a way to escape. And when she had no choice but to step into the nearby torchlight flickering from the sconce, she lowered her gaze to the floor. The clamor of fighting resounded from downstairs, still too far away for her to call to her brother for help.

She had no choice but to fight.

"Just one more," Poisoner cackled from the next room over. "I promise it won't hurt a bit."

The man's expression hardened as he lifted his sword and held the tip to her breast, seeming to realize she wasn't Poisoner at all. She backed up until the door standing between her and the man she loved blocked her way of escape. Her fingers searched in vain for the door handle, and when her hand closed around the latch, she pulled.

It was locked.

"Stop," Charles begged, coughing and spluttering through his pleading. "Stop!" His words escaped wet and slurred, as if his mouth fought against water. "I already gave you what you wanted. Now let her go."

Poisoner laughed. "I never intended to allow her to live. You are a fool, Huntsman. And soon, she will join you in the grave." She laughed again. "Really soon."

All too quickly, the door's latch lifted. The door flew open, and she stumbled inside before crashing to the floor in a heap of metal, weapons, and armor.

The enemy stood only a couple paces away, but despite the immediate danger, Emmaline searched for Charles with frantic eyes. She noted the small room with tables and shelves filled with books, ingredients, and more glass vials than she could count. A variety of substances ranging in color filled bowls and vials and jars.

But what she didn't see was Charles.

Instead, another wooden door lay closed in front of her, likely leading to where she wanted to go.

Emmaline scrambled to her feet, and Poisoner didn't stop her as she drew her dagger and held it between them.

"Very clever," Poisoner mused, flashing a dark, dangerous smile. "I ordered my men to kill you on sight. But I never expected *this*." The woman lifted a hand as if to touch her, fascination in her expression. "It's like looking into a mirror. A flawless execution of my identity." Her expression fell into a scowl. "Your talent is wasted in the grave. Fool of a king."

"Where is Charles?" Emmaline snarled, spinning around and swiping at the mercenary when he came too close. She missed and turned back to Poisoner.

The other woman nodded her head to the room behind her. "He's currently trapped in the agony of his own mind, dying a slow and painful death."

A gurgled cry rang out, muffled through the door. A sob climbed her throat and stuck fast to its inner walls. Charles! She needed to get to him. She couldn't let him suffer any longer.

She lowered her gaze to the ground, feigning loss and submission. "My talent need not waste away in the grave. Release him, and I will give myself to your service."

She turned her dagger around, careful not to nick herself, and offered her small blade to Poisoner.

"Only a scratch, no more." Bear's voice tugged at her mind as she recalled his words. *"Whatever you do, do not prick yourself."*

"Tempting offer," Poisoner mused, looking her up and down. "Oh, how I dislike wasting resources. Especially good ones." She clicked her tongue and shook her head. "Unfortunately, you will find Charles is not so easily swayed. He would only be a thorn in my backside should I do as you request."

All too suddenly, Poisoner grabbed her by the belt and pulled her closer, too fast for Emmaline to react. The woman's fingers closed around the antidote hidden in her pocket. And with a horrified expression, she could only watch as Poisoner threw the vial onto the ground, the glass shattering and the liquid antidote dispersing into the divots and grooves of the stone floor.

"Do not think me so easily fooled," Poisoner hissed as she snatched her poisoned dagger next, tossing it to the side. "I live up to my name. And your pathetic attempt at a rescue?" The woman's laugh echoed off the walls of the room. "If my hired men don't finish off your comrades... Then I will."

Poisoner pushed Emmaline with a forceful shove, and unused to wearing armor for any length of time, she stumbled beneath the weight of it and crashed to the ground. The other woman wasted no time before kicking her hard in the side. The armor took the brunt of the metal-line boot. But the air still whooshed from her lungs and her side flared with agony.

"Pathetic," Poisoner mumbled, turning her back to her. "You were easy enough to control at the Leonian palace. It will be no different here." To her hired guard, she said, "Lock her up for now. At least until Charles takes his last breath. I'll deal with her later."

"Wait!" Emmaline cried as she struggled onto her hands and knees. The chaos from below the stairs was getting louder. All she had to do was stall long enough to give herself a fighting chance. And in a raspy, breathless voice, she said, "I know the location of Armandy's heir."

That caused Poisoner to pause in her tracks and slowly turn back around. "Oh, I know several well-paying nobility who would kill for such information." She grabbed Emmaline by her breastplate and lifted her with inhuman strength. "Where is Christopher Avington?"

Emmaline opened her mouth to speak, but no sound came out.

"You must speak louder," Poisoner cackled, leaning closer. "I cannot hear you."

When the nasty woman moved the slightest bit closer, Emmaline's fingers closed around the knife hidden in her sleeve and stabbed upward.

Poisoner attempted to jerk backward, but this time, she wasn't fast enough as the knife nicked her beneath the chin, drawing out a trail of blood. The poison must have acted immediately, as Poisoner shrieked as she dropped Emmaline and stumbled backward.

The mercenary behind her stalked forward and swung his sword. Emmaline couldn't move fast enough, forcing her armor to take the blow to the stomach. Her armor dented but didn't break.

Another strike stabbed toward her. She leaped out of the way, all while glass shattered behind her as if Poisoner was trying to find a cure for being poisoned, throwing everything to the floor in her haste.

The next strike hit her arm and not only dented her armor but sliced through it enough to draw blood.

Emmaline dove between the mercenary's legs when he came at her again. And with a twist of her torso, she plunged her knife into the man's back, right where Charles had been stabbed earlier.

Perhaps he was unluckier, but he swayed on his feet before pitching forward and hitting the ground with a sickening thud. He didn't get up again.

Poisoner screamed hysterically as white foam flew out of her mouth. Her eyes were bloodshot, and a red rash climbed up her neck and settled in her face. She downed the contents of one of her vials. When it didn't seem to do the trick, she downed another.

Her lips turned blue. Her skin became unnaturally pale.

She bent over, her body spasming. But even through the jerky movement, the woman reached for her sword and charged toward Emmaline, weapon raised.

Emmaline rolled out of the way. And just when she expected another attack, a rock flung through the air and crashed into Poisoner's head.

The woman lost all control of her spasming body. And with her succumbing to the poison and whatever else she may have consumed, Emmaline rolled to her feet and rushed toward the closed door on the opposite side of the room.

She wrenched the door open.

And her stomach dropped to her throat.

Charles lay in a coffin made of glass. A hose reaching from one side of the room to the other was stuffed into one of the holes in the coffin, and water was quickly filling it up.

Forget the poison. Charles was drowning.

Chapter Nineteen

The world spun.

And the world was pain. It was fire. It was absolute misery.

How much time had passed? Charles couldn't recall the lapse of time through his hazy memory, his foggy mind, and the pain coursing through his body.

Panic consumed him and wrapped his mind in complete terror as the glass coffin filled higher and higher with water. He'd never been afraid of enclosed spaces. Until now.

With weak, feeble attempts, Charles kicked at the glass and slammed his fists into the hard, translucent surface over his head. Water continued to rise, fed through the holes near his feet where he couldn't reach.

His head burned. His body shivered. It was as if his muscles had lost all strength when poison coursed through his blood.

Still, he fought to escape.

Hard as he tried, his attempts proved futile.

Alarm clawed at his throat as each breath struggled into his lungs. A heaviness sat on his chest, making drawing air difficult. His breaths came quick, too quick, as he shifted his attempts to escape to an endeavor to survive.

He moved closer to the holes overhead and tried to calm the panic burning through his mind. Water continued to rise, lapping at his shoulders and then his neck. He barely managed to breathe through the remaining air pocket as the water reached his ears.

"Charles!" someone screamed on the opposite side of the room.

He turned his head just enough to catch a glimpse of black hair and a cruel, terrible face. But despite her features, he recognized the way she moved, the sound of her voice, the very expressions giving away her emotions.

The face was wrong, but he would recognize those blue eyes anywhere.

*Emmaline…*was his last thought before he gasped for one last breath, and then the water consumed him completely.

"Charles!" Emmaline gasped. She threw down her weapon and tore off her heavy gauntlets as she rushed toward the glass coffin filled with water.

Heart racing in her throat, she picked up a lone metal pole and cried out as she smashed it against the glass. Flecks chipped off, but otherwise, the glass didn't break.

Again and again, she hit the coffin, tears spilling from her eyes when it was too thick to crack under the duress of her best attempts. More glass chipped away. Charles' body ceased moving and became still.

"No!" she screamed. She smashed the metal against glass with every screech of the word. "No! No! No!"

It was too thick, and she resorted to trying to push the table the coffin lay on over to break the glass upon impact with the ground. But no matter how hard she pushed, it was too heavy to move.

"Stay back," Oliver ordered before pushing her out of the way. He lifted a mace over his head and brought it down swiftly on the coffin with a resounding crack. Glass shattered. Water spilled onto the floor.

Oliver heaved Charles out of the coffin and lowered him to the ground. She rushed to his side, frantic hands fluttering over his soaking form.

"He's not breathing!" she gasped, noting his closed eyes and the way his chest lay still. "He's not breathing!"

She slammed her fist between his shoulder blades. Once. Twice. And on the third time, Charles gasped in air and choked and spluttered, water spurting from his lips as she pushed him onto his side to help him expel the liquid.

He groaned and squeezed his eyes shut. His breaths escaped as raspy shudders. His body shivered from head to toe. His face was pale, his lips blue.

Without hesitation, she gathered him in her arms, lowered her head, and kissed him to offer what little of the antidote remained on her lips. She didn't know if he needed it, nor if it would work, but she had to try.

She broke the kiss, and after a minute, the raspiness of his breaths eased and his lips transitioned to a pinker hue while his skin took on a bit more color.

Oliver threw a blanket over his shoulders, which helped calm his shivering limbs. Not all the way, but enough.

"I'm so sorry we didn't arrive sooner," she murmured, resting her forehead against his.

He opened his mouth to speak, but when nothing escaped, he weakly wrapped an arm around her shoulders and held her close.

Bear rushed into the room with the other dwarves behind him, and the moment he laid eyes on them, he hobbled in their direction, knelt down, and pressed the spare vial of the antidote to Charles' lips.

The man didn't ask questions. He simply drank before sagging against her. She held him close, rocking him back and forth while thanking the stars that he was alive. She'd almost lost him.

"I thought she had you," he finally rasped, his voice hardly audible in its weak state.

She shook her head and brushed his damp hair away from his eyes. "Oh, she certainly promised to come back to hunt me down. But I think she lacked the manpower to do so immediately." Her face crumpled. "Forgive me for leading her to your residence. I should have been more careful."

"It's not your fault." He turned his head more fully into her shoulder. "I should have been more prepared for her to find me. I was careless."

"How were we to know the stab wound I gave her didn't deter her?"

He didn't answer, but rather breathed heavily into her shoulder as if it were all he could do to stay conscious.

A frown pulled on her lips as her gaze lifted to the coffin on the table, shards of glass of all sizes scattered across the ground. What a terrible way to die… Trapped. Poisoned. With no hope for escape.

When she attempted to stand, wanting to find the poor man a set of dry clothes, he clung to her tighter, as if she was his only anchor to life, to reality.

She soothed her hand up and down his back in an attempt to rub warmth into him. She met Oliver's eye where he approached with a second blanket, only to drape it over the first one. He wore a hard expression, one filled with anger and concern. She'd seen it plenty of times as they'd grown up together. A desire for justice. To protect those within his circle. His family.

"Charles," she murmured, stroking his damp hair. "We need to get you home. You need food. Warmth. Safety. It's not safe here."

Although by now, if the poisoned knife hadn't finished Poisoner off, the others would have.

"Mmm…" He inhaled a long breath and let it out slowly before his eyes fluttered open to reveal a haze of disorientation. "You wear another face, but I would recognize you anywhere."

She chuckled as she smoothed back his hair. "I finally took your advice and changed my hair color."

He grunted, and she didn't miss the flicker of a frown passing across his lips.

"It's only mud," she teased, poking him in the side. "It washes out."

"I think he likes your sunshine gold," Skippy laughed, tucking his fingers into his belt.

Oliver rolled his eyes. "You think?" But then he squeezed Charles' shoulder. "I hope you have room for seven more guests."

He didn't answer, as if he were too exhausted to reply.

Concern passed between her and her brother at his non-response. Another frown settled on her mouth as she felt his forehead. Hot. Too hot.

"Bear, what if that wasn't the right antidote?"

"It was the correct one for the poisoned apple." The smaller man crouched before Charles and assessed him. "I believe he may have been poisoned several times. Get him on home while we search for what toxins might have been used."

"What if his health declines?" Her frantic gaze fluttered over Charles. He appeared much improved since the last antidote, but his fever was worsening.

Bear squeezed her hand. "Trust us. We will do whatever it takes to help him."

After a long pause, she finally nodded and allowed the others, but mostly Oliver, to transport Charles outside and heave him onto a waiting horse with her brother holding him steady. She mounted her own next, and together, they sped off in the direction of Charles' estate, this time making sure no one followed them. They took several back roads just in case.

When they reached his residence in the darkness of early morning, they left the horses in the stables and supported Charles on either side as they entered the house. Rather than attempting to half-drag his heavy, muscled form up a flight of stairs, they helped him to the master bedroom and laid him on top of the bed.

Emmaline left the room for Oliver to strip him of his wet clothing and change him into something warmer. When her hands needed something to keep her busy, she made a hot pot of broth in the kitchen, bringing it, along with a glass of water, to his room when she was readmitted.

When he was too exhausted, feverish, and disoriented to care for himself, she spoon-fed him the broth while keeping his forehead cool with a damp cloth.

"These things don't usually happen," Charles insisted feebly, eyes unfocused. "Please don't reconsider."

She wrung the cloth out the window before dunking it in cool water to start again, resting it over his forehead. "I haven't changed my mind about accepting your proposal, Charles, and I never will."

She sat beside him on the bed, wishing she could take away his suffering. Only hours ago, each of them had been anticipating a fun, and perhaps competitive, game for her hand. And now? She worried she might lose him.

Taking a deep, steadying breath to calm her fears, she continued her administration, hoping to bring his fever down. And at the very least, keep it from climbing higher.

When he grunted, she lifted her head to find him staring at her with eyes slightly more focused than minutes earlier. "How strange..." he mumbled. "Your work is flawless. It's uncanny."

Only then did she realize she still wore Poisoner's face. But he didn't seem unsettled by it, nor did he ask her to take it off. He only watched her curiously while running a thumb in circles on the back of her hand.

"My talent occasionally comes in handy," she replied in a teasing tone to lighten the dark mood.

He only took a deep breath and let it out slowly as his eyes unfocused even more. She felt his forehead. His fever was climbing.

However, minutes later, her brother entered the room with the seven dwarves in tow. Bear administered several drops of two different elixirs to Charles. Over the next several hours, he shifted in and out of consciousness. At one point, shivers wracked his entire frame, and perspiration dripped down his face.

But they worked tirelessly through the day to bring down his fever and to eradicate his chills. Blessedly, as the sunset light filtered through the windows and bathed the room in an orange and pink glow, his fever finally subsided, and he slept soundly beneath the bed sheets.

She released a sigh of gratitude as she wearily left the room to clean the makeup from her face and the mud from her hair. She filled an empty wash bin and splashed cool water across her cheeks, wiping her face clean before settling in front of the hearth with her brother beside her in another armchair. The dwarves had left for the city to attend to business, and Godfrey was tucked away in his room down the hallway.

Fire crackled in the hearth, filling the ominous silence of what could have happened should they have reached Charles even a minute later. They didn't speak of it, but she knew it weighed on her brother's mind just as it did hers.

Her heart gave a start as she picked up the shuffling of feet down the hallway, and moments later, Charles appeared with a blanket wrapped around his shoulders, his face still pale from recovering.

"Charles!" she gasped, shooting to her feet. "You should be resting."

"I can't," he croaked as if speaking proved difficult. "I am plagued with knowing I don't fully have you."

"I don't know what you mean." She guided him to a wooden chair. "I'm right here."

"He means the card game," Oliver said, frowning as he tapped his fingers on top of his chair's armrests.

She shook her head. "Recovering from your ordeal should be your priority."

Charles' gaze roamed over her, lingering on her face she'd cleaned recently. "You are my priority."

Despite the fire billowing, reaching out with warming hands, he wore a heavy fur blanket around his shoulders, shivering as if he couldn't get warm no matter his efforts.

"Deal the cards," he said weakly to her brother.

Oliver's expression pinched, his lips pressing together. "You already have my blessing. You don't need to play."

"I want to. I want to be worthy."

"You already are."

"Please," was all he said.

Oliver and Emmaline shared a look of uncertainty. What Charles needed was rest. He'd almost died a horrific, poisonous death.

But if this was what he felt like he needed…

His expression still pinched, Oliver finally shuffled and dealt the cards between the two.

Charles hacked a cough, the sound muffled by his blanket. When the seizure of his lungs ended, he leaned back against his chair as if exhausted. It hurt to see him so…weak. So vulnerable. Experiencing so much misery.

Softly, she cradled his cheek in her hand and brushed her thumb along his cheekbone. "Rest, Charles. You can play when you feel stronger."

He rested his hand on top of hers and squeezed. "I can't lose you." His voice broke.

"I'm not going anywhere."

"You don't know that. I need to marry you. So I can protect you." He weakly nodded toward the cards. "And I want to do it right."

"You don't need to prove anything."

"I have everything to prove." His words cracked with despair. "I need to feel worthy of you." His shaky hand hid his expression as he paused for a moment before speaking again. "I cannot forgive myself for bringing you into this mess."

She pulled his face closer to bestow a gentle kiss upon his brow. "Did you forget how we met?" Laughter escaped her, eyes sparkling with amusement. "*I* brought *you* into this mess first. And we'll share in this messy mess together." She squeezed his hand. "We are partners, Charles. You can lean on me."

He closed his eyes and rested his head against her hand. "I need to do this, sweeting."

For a moment, her heart skipped in her chest, surprised at the name of endearment. What if he hadn't been acting during their little marriage charade? What if he had truly been fond of her all this time?

And then she realized this wasn't about his health. It wasn't about his pride, either. Considering his past...he needed the reassurance that he deserved to be a husband again. And later down the road, a father.

Therefore, she nodded, dropped her hand, and leaned back. He needed this. And she refused to stand in his way any longer.

Over the next hour, she drifted in and out of the room to supply Charles with water and light refreshments, easy on the stomach. He coughed and hacked and sniffled, his eyes glazed over as if he barely managed to remain upright. After an hour, she switched his chair to a softer cushion with armrests, which didn't seem to help him try his best to remain awake. But still, he played. Even as he lost the first game. And then the second. The third…

"I thought you said I should prepare to lose," Oliver taunted, but not without concern sparking in his eyes. He wasn't *completely* heartless when he played cards.

"I'm simply setting you up so you will lower your guard enough for me to win."

"At this rate, we'll be playing well into the morning."

Oliver set down his cards, a smirk growing across his face as if confident that he had won.

But then Charles laid down his hand before slumping back into the cushions, closing his eyes, and releasing a long breath. Within moments, his head rolled to the side and his breathing deepened with sleep.

"I can't believe it," Oliver chuckled, gesturing to the cards laid across the table. "He did it. And I didn't throw the game this time."

Emmaline tucked another blanket around Charles. The man didn't even stir, too exhausted from recovery to rouse from his sleep. He wasn't going anywhere anytime soon, that was for sure.

"You really love him." It wasn't a question but a statement.

"Yes," she swept a strand of hair out of his eyes, "I do."

Oliver busied himself with clearing the table of his cards and tucking them away in his pocket. "I knew someday we would have to go our separate ways. I didn't realize it would be so hard."

"Ollie." She patted his arm before he finally lifted his gaze. "We will still see each other often. I plan on performing with the troupe every summer." She grinned. "At least you won't have to scour Leonia to find me. You'll know exactly where I am."

"And I'll make sure to send word whenever the troupe moves, that way you will know exactly where we are." Her brother's eyes watered. "I hope you will find every happiness with him."

"I already do. He's everything to me."

Oliver's mouth lifted in a half-smile. "What a lucky man."

"What a lucky me, you mean."

He laughed quietly and pushed her shoulder teasingly. "Get some sleep." He lifted a warning eyebrow and added, "In your room."

She rolled her eyes. "You are no fun."

But he only chuckled and disappeared up the stairs.

Emmaline placed a soft kiss on Charles' forehead. Again, he didn't stir, and it broke her heart to have witnessed him suffer so much. But the danger had passed, and she had every faith that he would recover.

"I love you," she murmured, caressing his cheek.

He grunted in response, and she forced herself to keep from laughing. He certainly spoke an entire language through his grunts alone.

And she looked forward to discovering it all.

Chapter Twenty

Energy drained Charles' body with each of his sluggish movements as he finished dressing by buttoning his vest. He'd never wanted a valet more than in that moment, but he forged through the thick mud of fatigue and finished the ensemble with a variety of weapons hidden on his person.

One didn't meet a king with enough weapons to scare the man's personal guards, after all.

At least none that showed.

His legs felt heavy as he descended the length of the staircase, using the wall to help keep his balance. Banging pots and pans coming from the kitchen pulled his attention toward the open doors long enough to see a beautiful blonde-haired woman flitting by as she whisked something inside a bowl.

"Oh, do come eat, Charles!" she called to him. "You need to gain back your strength."

He perked up at the delicious smells wafting from the kitchen. Savory meat. Sweet bread. Tart jam. "You can cook?" he asked as his eyes widened with amazement at the spread of food on the table from sliced bread to strawberry jam to fruit cut up and displayed in an eye-catching manner on a plate.

"Mmhmm." She smiled before she stood on her toes and kissed his cheek. "I know it's likely not as good as you're used to, but—"

"Emma, you are incredible. I haven't had a home-cooked meal in…well, a long time. Godfrey doesn't cook, and I'm wary about allowing anyone else into my home."

Suddenly feeling ravenous, he sat down and inhaled the food far faster than what was deemed polite. But his body still felt terrible, so he would worry about manners another time.

He held up an apple slice. "Not poisoned?" It was meant to be a jest, and despite the terrible situation, he was grateful she played along.

"Not poisoned." She sat across from him and looked him up and down. "Where are you going?"

"To see the king." He glanced around, noting Oliver's absence. "Do you want to accompany me?"

Her lips pressed tight together as she twirled a strand of her curly hair around her finger. "The *king*? You make it sound like it's not a big deal."

"Because it's not. He's just a man."

"So says you. You grew up in such an environment."

Leaning forward with his hands clasped on the table, he explained, "You are going to have to be vetted, sweeting. Either I bring you to him, or he will send someone to me. I'd rather not have people lurking around the house, especially if I was gone."

She released a long breath. "I suppose it makes sense. No one will hurt me if you're not home, will they?"

He shook his head. "The king's men know to stay away from my property unless they want to find a knife in their throats. But I would like to take control of the situation if possible. If you are able to accompany me."

The chill running rampant in his body fled at the simple touch of her hand on his. "What do I have to do?"

"Nothing. He will likely quietly assess you rather than question you. And I will steer the conversation in your favor during my meeting with him."

She exhaled shakily. "Then let's go meet a king."

Together, and with more help than he wanted to accept from Godfrey, they prepared for their short journey to ride to the palace on horseback. She changed into a dress for the occasion. On the road, the fresh air filled his lungs with relief and soothed the lingering ache in his throat. But soon, his attention was captured by the awe in Emmaline's eyes as they entered the city of Edilann.

The kingdom's colors, blue and yellow, were splayed throughout the city from drapes to paint to the uniforms the soldiers wore as they patrolled. A cacophony of noises surrounded them on streets filled with horses, carts, shops, and more people than he could count.

Soon enough, they reached the palace gates, and recognizing him instantly, the two guards on either side lifted the gate to admit them entrance. The stable hand took their horses, and Charles linked his arm with Emmaline's to show they were more than mere acquaintances.

"I don't belong here," she murmured as they ascended the steps and entered the castle, trying to pull away from him.

He frowned. "We already had this discussion."

"I know. But… This is the palace. I could handle everything else just fine."

Thankfully, she didn't try to tug away again as a servant led them down blue-carpeted hallways boasting of intricate artwork, finely crafted furniture, and members of the court strolling about. The courtiers watched them curiously and quickly turned to gossip to their friends.

Their hushed voices disappeared when they turned another corner to find the king himself visiting with members of the court, the queen at his side.

Emmaline's grip tightened on his arm, her fingernails digging into his skin. Her breaths quickened, and he could feel her practically quaking in her slippers.

King Royce turned in their direction, and everyone around them hushed. Charles had hoped to have as few curious gossipers as possible during this interaction, but it looked as if they were about to jump headfirst into a dark tunnel, not knowing what lay on the other side.

Charles bowed at the waist, and Emmaline followed his example with a curtsy.

"Your Highnesses," he acknowledged.

The queen of gossipers herself snapped her fan closed and gave Emmaline an intense stare. "Who have you brought with you today, Sir Lockwood?"

He lifted her hand, showing off the blue gemstones on her finger. "My fiancée, Miss Emmaline Blythe." He made eye contact with the king, not to seek permission but to tell him this was his choice.

King Royce's eyes glinted with interest as if viewing her in a new light. "Where do you hail from?"

"Leonia," she answered in a meek tone.

"Ah. That reminds me, Sir Lockwood, that we have trading business to attend to. If you will excuse us."

Emmaline begged him with her eyes alone not to leave her, and he hoped he returned her concern with a look of reassurance before he followed the king down two more hallways, up a small flight of stairs, and into the square hallway housing the king's personal meeting rooms.

They entered one of them. King Royce drew back the drapes to let the light inside to reveal several bookshelves, an ornate table, and a variety of chairs situated around the table.

"Well?" King Royce asked without preamble. "Did you succeed?"

Unfortunately, Charles had learned the hard way not to question the king's motives, as he'd once lost the man's trust for a time before painstakingly earning it back. He knew not to ask about why he'd wanted Princess Isobel dead, but perhaps he might indulge the information naturally.

"A group of mercenaries beat me to the task, but I managed to escape with the princess in tow." His mind raced as he tried to weave a mixture of truth and falsehoods. "I weaseled some information out of her, only to realize she was a stand-in for the real princess."

The king leaned forward in his chair and stared him down. "Where is the real princess?"

He must lie. To protect the girl not even come of age yet. "I don't know. All I know is the reason for the stand-in is she is with child. The Leonian king wanted to wait to switch Princess Isobel with the fake after the child was born."

The other man chuckled darkly and shook his head. "Oh, what a clever trick. So many wanted the princess dead to prevent the marriage and have the king's reign end with him, including myself. I had a strategic alliance in place…"

He trailed off as if not wanting to divulge more information to his spy than he ought to. "And what happened to the girl? To the fake?"

Charles shuffled his feet, not even feigning his horror as he recalled the enemy's blade against Emmaline's throat, his desperation to save her life, and how the weapon had sliced into her throat. She had survived, but only barely.

"She was killed," he lied. "I managed to take down two of their men before I fled, leaving her body to the wolves." His eyebrows furrowed as he stared at his feet. "I wish I managed to get more information out of her before the attack, but I got as much as I could."

Although he was grateful for the Edilann king for allowing him to stay in the kingdom, giving him a job, and providing him safety from his kin in Armandy, the man was still a king who only had interests for himself. Charles needed to look after his own interests, which included his family and his friends.

No one could know Emmaline had been the fake. *No one.*

Otherwise, she would never be safe. King Royce needed to believe she was dead.

"And your fiancée?" King Royce asked carefully. "Where did you pick her up?" His eyes glinted knowingly. "She looks an awful lot like Princess Isobel."

He leaned casually against the table between them.

"I haven't seen the real princess, so I wouldn't know." Charles' eyes sparkled with feigned humor. "Poisoner attacked me on my way back to Edilann. I was saved by dwarves. They brought me back to their home, which is where

I met Emmaline. Any resemblance to the princess is purely coincidental."

Please believe me, he internally begged without betraying his rising fear.

Rather than commenting more about his fiancée, the king's eyes snapped open wide. "Poisoner? She's dead."

"She is now. She faked her death as your spy because she was already working for the Leonian king."

"A double-crosser?" the king growled. "Are you certain?"

"She told me herself."

"Is she connected to any of my other spies?"

"Not that I know of."

"I need you to find out. Stealthily, of course. This is your next assignment."

Charles nodded, glad he had so much of the king's trust to allow him to move freely among the upper class. "I will be getting married first, and then I will complete the assignment."

He wasn't asking permission. This marriage was happening even if King Royce disliked it. He didn't know whether the king would look into Emmaline's background, but she had nothing to hide that he could easily gain access to.

King Royce waved his hand with understanding before turning back to his task, a dismissal to leave. He didn't seem upset to have to wait a little longer. He just looked…tired. He didn't envy him his position. In fact, he was relieved because it was what he would have faced as the king should he have stayed in Armandy.

With one last dip of his head, he exited the room.

Only to stop short when he found young Prince Sterling standing outside the door, his striking blue eyes wide as he stared back at him. The eleven-year-old boy likely couldn't have overheard the conversation within the room, but he'd always believed the prince possessed keen eyes and ears.

Charles bowed slightly at the waist to acknowledge him and continued on his way, all too aware of the boy's gaze probing into his back. Currently, he was King Royce's spy. And one day, he would be Sterling's.

As he made his way down the hallway, he smiled softly as he straightened his sleeves. He had a wedding to plan.

Chapter Twenty-one

Flower petals rained over their heads in an array of yellows, pinks, whites, and blues. Charles pulled Emmaline into a kiss to seal their marriage as husband and wife while their friends and family cheered loudly around them.

She laughed joyfully as her new husband pulled her in for another kiss and another until her legs wobbled with pure happiness.

"I said only one kiss!" Oliver shouted from the crowd.

But she only laughed against Charles' smiling lips, hardly believing the journey and trials they'd endured to stand beneath the arch of matrimony and vow to love and cherish each other to the end of time.

Music struck up around them, lively and happy and intoxicating while their audience continued to cheer and clap wildly when they held up their intertwined hands.

Emmaline beamed at her beloved family standing in the crowd beneath a sunny afternoon sky, each supporting her with her next grand adventure. Charles' friends bellowed with congratulations. The sight of so many loved ones supporting them brought warmth to her heart.

"Dance with me!" she laughed as the crowd formed into lines for the first set. But as she tugged Charles forward, he planted his feet like an immovable tree with roots burrowed deep within stubbornness and denial.

"I don't dance."

"It's easy. I'll teach you."

He shook his head, his lips thinning as he stared at the dancers waiting for them. "I've had more dance lessons than you can count. I am perfectly able to dance. I just don't like it."

Ah. She understood now. Dancing reminded him of who he used to be, and he wanted to forsake that identity entirely.

She gently squeezed his hand. "This is no stuffy ballroom swaying, soldier." Her lips pulled up in a grin at her jest. "Indulge your wife one dance, and then you can brood to your heart's content."

His lips twitched as if he tried not to smile, and finally, he pulled up his roots and allowed her to lead him in the first line dance. One dance became two. Two became three. Until they danced for what felt like hours until the sun descended upon the distant horizon.

Charles took her by surprise by swinging her out of the line, and she couldn't help but giggle with giddiness when he led her by the hand into the dim shadows of the trees. She doubted their sudden disappearance went unnoticed. But no one stopped them. Not even Oliver. Her brother was too busy drinking and dancing and wooing to seemingly care.

"How much is it to ask for solitude with my own wife?" he asked in a husky tone, one that made her toes curl and for pleasant shivers to race down her arms.

He trapped her against a nearby tree and kissed her until her knees weakened and she could scarcely breathe.

Only when he moved his administration from her lips to her jaw and then her throat did she manage to speak. But barely. Especially when his mouth created hot trails of passion in its wake.

"Oh, I do like the sound of that title."

"Better than 'princess,' eh?"

She gasped when he kissed her collar bone and planted tender kisses along her neck to her ear. "Much better. I am quite happy to call myself your wife."

He stopped kissing her long enough to trap her face in his hands and gaze at her with such longing and love and warmth in his expression to steal the breath from her. "You have no idea how much it means to hear you say that."

Resting her hands over his, she turned her head to kiss his palm. "I will say it for the rest of our days together, Charles."

He pulled her closer until she found herself wrapped up in the safety of his strong, sturdy embrace. She sighed contentedly, holding him around the waist and resting her head against his chest. The safety he offered wrapped her in a warm cocoon of happiness, knowing he would take care of her heart, body, and soul.

"I'm a lucky man," he murmured against her hair.

"I'm not sure how much luck had to do with you rescuing me from certain death." She kissed his chest, and he responded by holding her tighter. "It seems more like fate."

"Fate…" She felt him smile against her, and he held her even closer before planting a kiss on her head. "I like the sound of that."

Epilogue

Charles paced back and forth across the length of the hallway, nearly tearing his hair out with each of his wife's screams. Every fiber of his body demanded to kick down the doors to their bedroom, but he'd already been escorted out several times by infuriating midwives who insisted the birthing room was no place for a man.

"Just knowing you are outside the door is all the comfort I need," Emmaline had said to reassure him.

But it wasn't enough. He needed to hold her hand, to tell her everything was going to be alright.

Or perhaps, he was the one who needed reassurance. What if he lost her? What if he lost the baby? He couldn't experience such grief again. He was certain such agonizing heartache would kill him—

A high-pitched cry broke him out of his anxious thoughts. The shock of the sound caused him to stumble backward until he landed on the bottom stair with a disbelieving thump. He stared at the closed doors, blinking several times in shock.

Little by little, the baby's cries transitioned from wailing to whimpers until no sound came from the room at all aside from the hushed whispers of the midwives. He held his breath, his heart pounding as he waited for the doors to open, to admit him into the room. To find out…

To find out if his wife still lived.

Finally, one of the midwives opened the door and smiled, gesturing him inside.

He pushed himself off the stair and bounded into the room, his gaze searching for a head of blonde hair. He found Emmaline lying beneath piles of clean sheets on the bed, holding a bundle in her arms.

"Charles," Emmaline laugh-sobbed, exhaustion in every facet of her expression.

Several long strides carried him across the room and to her side. He cradled her face in his hands and gave her a long, lingering kiss full of love and gratitude. She was alive. Oh, how he'd feared for nine months that she wouldn't make it to the end. Not because of her health, but because of the terror of his past.

"What is it?" he murmured when he broke away from her, his gaze shifting to the wet, matted blond hair peeking out from a yellow blanket.

"A boy." She beamed at him, pride over what she'd accomplished shining in her eyes. "Would you like to hold him?"

Wordlessly, he reached out for the bundle, and she carefully transferred the babe to his arms. The small child whimpered as if he disliked being away from his mother, but after a few bounces, the child closed his eyes once more and settled into sleep.

"He's beautiful," he murmured, bestowing a kiss upon the soft skin of his forehead. "Our son."

And then his gaze frantically found Emmaline, as if letting her out of his sight for a single moment might take her away from him. But she was whole and healthy and smiling.

"I'm still here," she reassured, reaching out to squeeze his arm. "I will always be here."

He knew that, but he feared it might take a bit more time to truly believe it.

He climbed on the bed beside her, and together they held their son between them as the midwives worked around the room. The babe looked as if he might have curly hair, and the shape of his chin reminded him of his wife.

Emmaline smiled softly as she ran a finger over the baby's plump cheek. "Those are most certainly your ears."

"Are they?"

"Mmhmm." She leaned her head against his shoulder as if too exhausted to do anything other than snuggle into his side. "I am so happy, Charles. Getting rescued by a handsome man with a helmet stuck to his head was the best thing to have ever happened to me."

A chuckle escaped him as he remembered the incident clearly. "I would still be walking around with it stuck to my head if not for you."

"Indeed, you would," she teased.

Their attention turned to their sweet boy as he cooed in his sleep. It felt...surreal to hold him in his arms. Alive and well. Plump and healthy. At one point in his life, he'd convinced himself he'd never allow himself another wife, and he'd never have more children.

He was immensely glad he'd broken his vow to himself because this beautiful family in his arms, *his* family, was the greatest blessing in his life.

"What shall we name him?" she asked tiredly.

"It was tradition to name children after family where I come from. But…" He shook his head and turned to look at his wife. "I cannot. Perhaps you might name him."

Another smile graced her lips, and just the sight inspired him to wrap his arm around her to pull her closer, to feel her solid presence against his side if only to know she was real and tangible and with him. Always.

"What if we name him after my father? Phillip Lockwood."

"It's perfect." He kissed their son on his forehead before kissing Emmaline, too. "It's absolutely perfect."

ABOUT THE AUTHOR

Sydney Winward is an award-winning fantasy and paranormal romance author who dabbles in the occasional historical fiction. She loves building complex worlds filled with magic, strong characters, and emotional stories that can make you laugh and cry.

Sydney is the author of the Sunlight and Shadows Series and the best-selling Bloodborn Series, and when she's not writing, she's reading, thinking about stories, or going on adventures with her children. She lives in Utah with her husband and three amazing kids.

www.sydneywinward.com